Choosing someone to murder was not as difficult as Jennifer thought it would be. The first criterion was obvious: the world must improve with the victim's absence. Second, she felt the death should be symbolic for all those poor souls struggling to publish the masterpieces that no one would ever read because of someone else's whim. Third, she felt an obligation that the victim be childless and preferably spouseless. Fourth, he or she must be a true career S.O.B.

The answer was obvious: local lout and literary agent Penney Richmond. . . .

DYING TO GET PUBLISHED

Judy Fitzwater

FAWCETT CREST • NEW YORK

A Fawcett Crest Book
Published by The Ballantine Publishing Group
Copyright © 1998 by Judy Fitzwater

http://www.randomhouse.com

Library of Congress Catalog Card Number: 97-97182

ISBN 0-449-00294-2

Manufactured in the United States of America

First Edition: September 1998

10 9 8 7 6 5 4 3 2 1

For my mother and father,
who taught me that anything is possible.
And for my husband, Larry,
who shared this and all my dreams.

Many thanks to my husband, Larry, and my daughters, Miellyn and Anastasia, my first and best critics and the ones who have ridden the crests of my joys and endured the depths of my disappointments.

To my dear friends and fellow writers Deborah Barnhart and Celeste Duplaa for their undying support and incredible insight.

To my critique group: Robyn Amos, Barbara Cummings, Ann Kline, Barbi Richardson, and Vicki Singer, without whose help, encouragement, and wonderful talent this book would never have been written.

To the members of my writers' workshop who were with me every step of the way, especially Bob Bockting, Matt Perriens, and Olivia Suszynski, whose generosity I will never forget.

To Malinda Lo, who read this book and recommended that it be bought.

And to my editor, Joe Blades, whose kindness, good humor, and patience have made getting published delightful rather than deadly.

DYING
TO GET
PUBLISHED

Chapter 1

The jail cell was cold. Cold and gray and ugly. Jennifer ran her hands through her long, taffy-brown hair and sank wistfully against the wall. The chill reached through her sweater and embraced her shoulders. She shot straight up on the backless bench and shivered. She felt as though something were crawling down her back, something with many legs, but she knew it was her imagination. She prayed it was her imagination.

She thanked God that she was alone in the cell—no gun moll, no whore in wig and fishnet stockings, no runaway street kid whose innocence had just been ravaged. She knew them all so well, but not in the flesh, never in the flesh.

She wondered how she had come to such a state, how she would ever explain to Sam or Dee Dee or Mrs. Walker. Or anyone else she had ever known in her twenty-nine years.

And what would all this mean to Jaimie, her unborn child? She patted her stomach and sighed. She had promised Jaimie she (or was it he?) would someday be born. He (or she) had yet to be conceived. "Don't give up hope, little one," she whispered. "We've been through so much

1

together." Not for the first time, she wondered about her own sanity. She was talking to an unfertilized egg.

Jennifer would like to pretend that her arrest had been a complete misunderstanding. She didn't belong in a jail in Atlanta, Georgia. She'd only toyed with the idea of murder. A mere whim. An elaborate game.

Okay, so she'd planned the whole thing, but that wasn't the point. Except for a brief dalliance with Buddhism, she was a good Baptist girl. She knew right from wrong. The Ten Commandments were clear. They were even numbered for easy reference, and number six left no room to hedge.

And hadn't she promised God when she was immersed in the baptismal pool that, if He didn't let her drown, she would always be good? By the third dip she truly believed in miracles, and came up sputtering with a new understanding of what it was to be "reborn."

Jennifer Marsh was no more a murderer than Jimmy Carter was an adulterer. She was a caterer and a novelist—a mystery novelist. True, she had committed murder twelve times in eight novels—if you didn't count Sir Conrad's death, which turned out to be the result of natural causes. Eight novels that were stacked neatly on the shelf in her hall closet—eight novels collecting layers of dust—nearly three thousand manuscript pages.

Stacked next to them in a pile that seemed to tower over the manuscripts were rejections from some of the best publishing houses and most prestigious agents in the country. The story was always the same: "While your characters are interesting, I feel they are not unique enough to carry a series," or "I'm sorry but while your material is exceptionally well written and plotted, I could not become sufficiently enthused with it to take it on."

So they wanted unique. She gave them unique in her last book. Her heroine, Jolene Arizona, was a left-handed, blind-in-one-eye, bareback-riding circus performer turned Hollywood detective who took stunt gigs on the side when her client list dwindled. And she slept with all of them—every solitary client—employing a few tricks she'd learned on the circus circuit.

Jennifer sighed and settled back against the wall, letting the cold creep into her bones—she didn't deserve any better—and let her mind wander back to the day just three weeks ago when she set in motion the events that would inevitably lead to that cold jail cell: the day she decided to commit murder. . . .

As usual, she'd been hard at work, writing most of the morning. A little after eleven o'clock she typed the words THE END on page 293 of Jolene Arizona's first adventure. Tears of joy stung Jennifer's eyes. This one, she promised herself, this one would sell. The elation was suddenly washed away with a wave of nausea. She pushed back from the word processor and ran to the bathroom, where she stripped off her clothes and let the warm water of the shower flow over her, mingling with her tears. She would not sell her soul for a buck just to be published. She would not.

The roughness of the fresh towel brought her back to reality. She dried off, folded herself into the warmth of her royal blue terry-cloth robe, and wrapped the towel about her head. She caught her reflection in the mirror that ran the width of the small bathroom. She looked tired, bereft of vitality. Who was she fooling with her dreams of being a novelist? Maybe it was time to settle, time to make a little fire in the fireplace, time to clean the closet.

She sighed, wiped a final stray tear from her cheek and walked barefoot into the bedroom. The remote control was where it always was, between the pillows on the unmade double bed. She sank onto the sheets, not caring that the damp from the towel was seeping into the feather nest of her pillow. She touched the *on* button and the face of Geraldo Rivera loomed before her. Another show about prostitutes. How quaint.

She touched the *channel up* button and Sally's red glasses appeared on her smiling, blonde head. Nice work if you could get it—talking to people day after day who made you feel like you were so much better off than they. The topic was romance gone bad. What a unique idea!

Another flip of the button brought Oprah's smiling face into view. She was talking to an author. Jennifer lay paralyzed on the bed. *Turn it,* she ordered herself, but her finger lay still. *Turn it,* she demanded again, but it was fatally too late.

This was no celebrity book this woman was promoting. She had been unjustly accused of murdering her husband. The trial had been in all the papers. Jennifer remembered it vividly. It was such an involuted case, she'd clipped several of the articles for her idea file. But the woman had been exonerated. She was not guilty after all. Not only was she not guilty, she had written a book released just last week that was already in its third printing. She was famous, she was acquitted, and she was on her way to living happily ever after.

Jennifer pushed the power button and the screen went blank. Her eyes fuzzed out of focus, a nervous twitch settled into one corner of her mouth, pulling it upward into a half-crazed smile, and her thoughts . . . her thoughts strayed in a direction that would lead her straight to jail.

Chapter 2

Choosing someone to murder was not as difficult as Jennifer thought it would be. The first criterion was obvious: the world must improve with the victim's absence. Second, she felt the death should be symbolic for all those poor souls struggling to publish the masterpieces that no one would ever read because of someone else's whim. Third, she felt an obligation (for Jaimie's sake) that the victim be childless and preferably spouseless. Fourth, he or she must be a true career S.O.B.

Jennifer adjusted the bulky towel threatening to slide off her wet hair, pulled open the drawer of the file cabinet cramped in the back of her closet, and riffled through the file marked AGENTS. The rejection letters were neatly stacked on the shelf, but the lists of agents, names copied laboriously from lectures, professional newsletters, and *Literary Marketplace*, were all kept neatly within the file. Next to each name was a date and a notation reflecting their replies to her queries and sample chapters: FL, form letter; PR, personal reply; PRWP, personal reply with praise; and GAANWAW, which stood for Go Away and Never Write Another Word.

Most literary agents were polite. Some grew less polite

with time. Her eyes wandered to the name of one agent with half a dozen notations in the margin. Jennifer's stomach began to quease. She had spent more than a year in correspondence with Penney Richmond. First, the query that took three months for a reply, then another four for the glowing response to the first fifty pages of *The Corpse Found a Home*, her fourth novel, and finally another six months before she read those awful words: "I just didn't *love* it enough. I'm sure you'll have no trouble placing it. It's a great book." And a year older.

The phone call had been hell.

JENNIFER: "What was wrong with *The Corpse Found a Home*?"

PENNEY: "Let me see. I read so many things. Was that the book with the body that kept getting shuffled from one place to another?"

JENNIFER: "Yes. Four friends had gone out together, one died, and each of the other three thought something they did had killed him."

PENNEY: "Cute idea. It made me laugh. It would never sell. Everything is reality-based now—gritty."

JENNIFER: "Couldn't you tell it was funny from my query letter or at least the first fifty pages? You could have saved me nine months."

PENNEY: "I don't have time for this."

The phone clicked off.

The woman had tied up her manuscript for a year, and she couldn't give her five minutes on the phone—five minutes to vent some of the pressure that had been building for years—five minutes that now might have made Jennifer pass over her name on that list of agents. Instead, her finger tapped ominously in the margin. Penney Richmond met criterion number two; the death of an agent would certainly be symbolic for any struggling author.

Richmond was an Atlanta agent, which was perfect, little more than an hour and a half away from Macon. It would be a piece of cake to check out her family history. Maxie Malone, the sleuth in her first two novels, was a former actress with a talent for voices, and an expert at collecting information.

Jennifer slipped into the bedroom, clutching the paper with the agent's name and phone number. She sat down on the floor with her legs crossed and dialed the phone that lay on the walnut night table next to her bed. Muffy, the greyhound she'd saved from death after its racing days were over, nuzzled up against her on the floor.

"Richmond Literary Agency. How may I help you?" a voice asked.

"Ooooooh, *guten morgen*," she said in an exaggerated, singsong fashion. Muffy wedged her head between Jennifer's elbow and her side. "I was given this number. I'm Mrs. . . . Mrs. Smith's nanny." She winced, unsuccessfully trying to push Muffy aside. Silently, she cursed herself. Couldn't she come up with something more original? Probably not, with an emotionally needy greyhound at her side. "They are leaving the country for a year in Europe," she continued. "Frau Smith said Frau Richmond might need me."

The woman at the other end of the line began to laugh, first a titter that gave way to a guffaw. Jennifer felt the heat from her cheeks spread all the way to her navel.

"Boy, lady, have you got the wrong Richmond. *Ms.* Richmond doesn't have any children, bless their little unborn hearts, and she disposed of husband number three at least a dozen years ago."

"But surely she is the Frau Richmond who lives at that most lovely of places the . . . the Magnolia. . . ."

"Couldn't be the right one. Ms. Richmond lives downtown at O'Hara's Tara."

"So sorry to bother. Excuse the ring." Jennifer slapped the receiver back into its cradle, pushed the dog away, and crawled up onto the bed. It worked. It actually worked—just as easily as it had in her book. Maxie Malone would be proud.

No children. No spouse, although from the receptionist's reaction, a husband probably wouldn't have been a hindrance. He might have offered her a hand. Richmond met criterion number three.

She reached down, opened the top drawer of her nightstand, and extracted her address book. Tucked neatly in the front flap was a scrap of paper saved from a writers' convention she'd attended in Columbus. On it was scribbled the name and number of a multipublished author she'd met who generously suggested that she feel free to call with questions. She dialed the Savannah number. A pleasant voice answered the phone, and Jennifer asked to speak to Agnes Weathers.

"This is she," the pleasant voice answered.

"I know you don't remember me, but I met you at the Midnight Dreary Mystery Convention last fall in Columbus. I'm looking for an agent, and I thought perhaps you could offer me a bit of advice," she said in a tiny, breathy, little girl voice. She covered the mouthpiece with her hand and rolled her eyes. Where had that come from—"a bit of advice"? She sounded like someone from *Masterpiece Theatre*.

"Oh, dear. I'd like to help but I really can't recommend anyone to you unless I've seen your work, and I'm afraid I just don't have time—"

"Actually, I just wondered if you might give me your opinion of an agent I was considering approaching—Penney Richmond."

For a moment Jennifer thought the woman had hung up. "Are you there?" she asked.

"I don't know of any specific complaints about Penney. She certainly has never done anything illegal, such as fraud or withholding payment. At least not that I know of."

"I hear a *but*. What's the *but*?"

"You're new to the business?"

"Yes," she whispered in the innocent voice.

"Are you old enough to drink?"

"Why no, and I wouldn't even if I could. But I can vote."

"No one should be dealing with Penney Richmond unless they can have a stiff martini afterward. That woman will have you for breakfast. Stay away from her. There're too many good agents out there for you to get mixed up with her. And if you repeat any of this to anyone, I'll deny it." The phone went dead.

A smile twitched at the corners of Jennifer's mouth. She ignored the nibbles Muffy was directing at her bare toes dangling from the edge of the bed. She had something far more important on her mind. Penney Richmond passed condition four. She was a true career S.O.B.

Chapter 3

Jennifer grasped the sleek handle of the meat cleaver and lifted it above her head. In one swift, clean motion she brought it down, slicing through sinew and splattering the whiteness of her apron with blood.

"What a mess!" Dee Dee exclaimed. "Don't put so much strength into the blow. You need to keep most of the motion in the wrist. If you do, you won't get blood all over my kitchen."

She took the cleaver from Jennifer, picked up a large knife, and carefully sliced the boneless beef roast, placing each piece in a large baking pan.

"I told you I wasn't any good at this," Jennifer complained, wiping her hands on a paper towel.

"You're acting like a three-year-old. I bet you used to break the dishes to get out of washing them."

"I only tried it once. I didn't get an allowance for two months and I still had to do the dishes. But I never signed on to do beef. Our agreement was clear—I do most of the vegetables and appetizers; you take care of the meat and the potatoes. You can't expect a vegetarian to warm up to roasted flesh."

Dee Dee threw her a soapy dish rag. "We've only got four hours to get this order done. I'll throw the sauce on the beef, and you start on the vegetable tray. Our clients aren't vegetarians. They don't want any of your tofu or soy substitutes."

"Then they're barbarians."

"That's Mr. and Mrs. Big Bucks Barbarians to you, my dear friend. So get with it!"

Jennifer carefully blotted the blood with the wet rag. Was human blood so easy to clean up? A simple wipe and all evidence disappeared into the warm cloth, leaving a perfectly clean counter. If she could only catch Penney Richmond reclining on Formica.

"Are you doing the parsley wreath with carrot and radish roses and turnip daisies?" Dee Dee asked.

"You don't use both kinds of roses on the same wreath. It leads to sensory confusion. Roses have to taste the same. You give each vegetable the shape of a different flower."

"Fine. Whatever. Create and be done with it. I'll put the potatoes on to boil."

Jennifer took a twelve-inch foam ring, covered it in plastic wrap, and placed it atop a bed of lettuce on a silver tray. Deftly, she transformed the circle into a parsley wreath. She could make a larger one and drape it with a sash: REST IN PEACE, PENNEY. She could send it to the viewing and leave her card under the doily. The police would find it amusing, clever. They'd talk about her down at the precinct. That would be just the beginning of her fame.

But first she had to devise a plan to rid the world of Penney Richmond—a plan that would lead the police straight to her door and to her arrest. The hard part would be creating an alibi that would clear her of the crime.

She would be arrested, her name and face splashed

across every newspaper in the city. The wire services would pick it up. Tom Brokaw, Peter Jennings, and Dan Rather would utter her name in disbelief. An aspiring novelist, a victim of the system, had temporarily lost her mind. And then a week later—two, tops—the police would uncover irrefutable evidence that Jennifer Marsh could not have committed the crime. Unjustly accused, martyred for her cause, she'd be the hottest topic in the media. Her books would be published and sell wildly. She would be famous and all would be right with the world.

"You're plotting again, aren't you?" Dee Dee said. "Every time you start a new book, your eyes glaze over, you go deaf, and you fade into slow motion like one of those action heroes in a movie. Three o'clock—that's when the reception is—three o'clock—today—in four hours—you and me in those cute little white tuxedo shirts and black ties and black skirts. Got it?"

"I've got it. I've got it, already. I'm curling carrots, see? I'm putting them in ice water, see?"

"Come on, Jennifer. You've always got to make me out the bad guy. We need the work. Business has been really slow this winter."

"I don't mind it when business is slow."

"Of course you don't. You don't have a husband in a dead-end job or a daughter who takes piano and dance lessons. No clients means you have more time to write. But the books aren't bringing in any money, Jen, money for trivial things like rent, food, electric."

"I do all right."

"Jen, it's time to take a look at yourself. Writing is fine, but it can't be your whole life." Dee Dee spoke quietly, like a sage calling down to her from some high mountain.

Get off it, Jennifer thought. Dee Dee was only two years older than she.

"You owe it to yourself. You owe it . . ." Here it comes, Jennifer thought—Dee Dee's about to play her trump card. ". . . you owe it to Jaimie."

"Don't bring Jaimie into this!"

"Jaimie needs a father."

"Jaimie doesn't exist."

"You talk like it does."

"Don't call Jaimie an *it*."

"Just how do you expect me to deal with Jaimie's gender ambiguity? Jaimie needs a pronoun, and the only way for him, her, whatever, to get one is a process we call conception and birth—and that's one process you can't intellectualize. If that egg of yours doesn't meet the right sperm before it shrivels up, there will never be a Jaimie. You don't even date. You're always going to your critique group or to some writers' conference—that is, when you're not holed up in that depressing little apartment of yours typing away. The only time you get out is when you go on a job with me."

"Writing is something I've got to do. I don't know any other way to explain it."

"Then do it—just do something else, too. And keep yourself open to possibilities."

"What possibilities?"

"This wedding we're going to this afternoon. Weddings always have lots of eligible men. Promise me—just keep your options open."

Jennifer rolled her eyes. It'd be a cold day in hell before she picked up some man at a wedding.

Chapter 4

He was beautiful—tall, muscular, with chiseled features and a head of sandy blond hair—the most beautiful man Jennifer had ever seen. She could hardly take her eyes off him as the warm, afternoon sun made his hair sparkle.

"Have you ever seen anyone more gorgeous in your life?" she whispered to Dee Dee as they arranged canapés on four large, round trays at their shaded work station.

"I can't believe you!" Dee Dee sighed. "We cater a wedding and *you* fall in love with the groom. What kind of self-destructive behavior is that? But at least you're looking. I'm glad you're looking." She surveryed the wedding guests from the brick patio of the rolling ranch-style house.

"Can't you feel the electricity?"

"The only electricity you're feeling is a wayward spark from the very complete circuit that's running between the newlyweds. John Allen could have any woman he wants. Everyone knows that—including him—and he chose Lily Dawber, first runner-up in this year's Miss Georgia pageant."

"He looks even better in person than he does anchoring the news on Channel 14, don't you think?"

"He's hungry."

"What?"

"He's hungry. They're *all* hungry."

"How do you know that?"

"It says so right here on the order. Bride and groom arrive at reception site. Drinks and hors d'oeuvres served. The bride's family says they're hungry, so they're hungry. Don't blow this one for us, Jen. It's spring, an especially warm spring, and the beginning of the catering season. There're a lot of important people here—even if it is a small wedding. We could get jobs from this."

Jennifer shouldered a large platter and tacked on an artificial smile. "I'm smiling. I'm serving. I'll be back when the hungry hordes have devoured these delicacies."

She moved into the crowd clustered around the edge of the oval-shaped pool. Dee Dee was right. They were hungry. In less than five minutes she returned with her tray stripped of its contents and retrieved a second salver. "I just hope we brought enough with us," she said over her shoulder to Dee Dee. "They all act like they skipped lunch."

She headed out to a group chatting next to the cherry trees, which were in full bloom. "Canapé?" she asked. The cluster broke and regrouped with her at the center as they made their selections.

One distinguished-looking white-haired man, barely taller than Jennifer's five feet six inches, leaned close to her ear. "These are mighty good," he told her, taking a third sample. "Do you have a card?"

"I know you," she said, her eyes widening. "You're Steve Moore, twelve o'clock news."

The man smiled, the charming, worldly smile she had

seen so often on her TV set. "That's right, little darlin', and you are . . ."

"Jen, that is, Jennifer Marsh of DD Catering." She reached in the pocket of her skirt and pulled out a business card.

"And I can reach you here?"

"We offer a full range of services," she stated.

His face was a little too close to hers, and the smell of champagne on his breath suddenly engulfed her as he moved even closer to her shoulder. "You don't say."

Jennifer blushed hotly. "If you'll excuse me, I'll get some more canapés." She escaped back down the other side of the pool, where she offered two guests the last of the hors d'oeuvres.

As she headed back toward the work station, she heard a voice behind her.

"Moore scare you off? Don't let the rest of us starve because some old lech was breathing down your blouse."

The heat that was fading from her face returned with full force. She whirled, the tray almost clipping the ear of a dark-haired man who looked to be in his early thirties.

"Whoa! Watch it with that thing, will ya? I can just see the headline my editor would put on that story. 'Brash Reporter Decapitated by Beautiful Caterer Wielding Unbelievably Large Tray.' "

All of the blood in Jennifer's body had now accumulated in her cheeks. "Look, I'm really sorry. Did I hit you?"

"Just grazed me was all."

They stared at each other. There was something in those eyes, some mysterious inviting quality that said if she'd only give him a chance, she just might find him irresistible.

Fat chance! she thought and turned to head back to Dee Dee.

"You should watch out for Moore," he called after her, catching up to her side. "He's got a reputation for using his status as a TV anchor and that perfect smile to impress the ladies."

"You needn't worry. I'm not easily impressed."

"So I noticed."

She dropped the tray onto the table next to Dee Dee, who was frantically spreading cream cheese on tiny bits of bread. The other three trays sat full.

Jennifer pulled at the elasticized bow tie at her neck. It plopped back into place. "What do you think about getting some other uniforms—something a little less revealing?"

Dee Dee stared at the crisp, pleated tuxedo shirt that was buttoned all the way up to the mandarin collar. "What did you have in mind? A gunnysack? You're an attractive woman, Jennifer, and there's nothing more appealing to a man than a woman offering food. Who was hitting on you this time?"

"Some old man from TV," she grumbled.

"And who's your friend that followed you home?" Dee Dee asked.

"Sam Culpepper, *Macon Telegraph*." He extended his hand toward Dee Dee. She opened hers. It was smeared with spiced cream cheese.

"Sorry. Dee Dee Ivers."

"You feed them," Jennifer interrupted. "I'll spread cream cheese and you feed them."

"All right," Dee Dee agreed, wiping her hands on a towel. "We'll open the buffet in about forty minutes. We only need one more tray full. And don't forget to add the prosciutto."

Dee Dee hefted a platter onto her shoulder and took off toward the crowd.

"I'd be glad to help," Sam offered.

"You can't. You're not licensed, and you haven't had a TB test." Jennifer slapped the spread onto a small rectangle of bread, added black olive slices, rolled it up, and stuck a toothpick through it.

"You forgot the ham," Sam said.

"No, I didn't," Jennifer assured him.

"You're not really a caterer, are you?" he asked.

She stopped and stared at him. "Of course I am," she stated emphatically before returning to the tiny sandwiches. "Why did you say that?"

"It seems to me this is probably the last place you'd like to be right now."

"Did you consider it might be the company and not the job?"

He laughed. "Could be, but that plastic smile you sport when you're serving is a giveaway. You're far too easy to read."

"And I suppose you're an expert on reading people."

"It's my job."

"You don't say."

"The best skill an investigative reporter can have is being able to tell when someone is telling the truth."

"Then see if you can decipher this: I've got work to do, and I'd really rather you'd just leave."

"Sure. That one is easy: you're telling me that you find me incredibly attractive, and you'd love to have dinner with me Friday night."

She looked him up and down and sighed. "Why do I feel like I just stepped into an enormous wad of bubble gum?"

Chapter 5

"A gun? You're planning to kill that woman with a gun? How mundane!" Leigh Ann pouted like a child who had been denied a lollipop. "How could you do that to us, Jennifer? Half the fun of coming to this writing group every Monday night is finding out how you're going to rub out your next victim." She pushed her brunette locks behind her ears, stuffed a handful of pretzels into her mouth, and settled her petite frame onto the over-stuffed sofa.

"Oh, I don't know. I come to see how your bad-boy hero is going to seduce your virginal young heroine—yet again," Jennifer countered.

"You just don't appreciate the romance in life," Leigh Ann complained. "Relationships are what living is all about, but then I guess you—"

"This gun thing—it's just not your style, Jen," Teri chimed in, stretching out her long, coffee-colored legs in front of her on the floor, grabbing her ankles and doing little, dancerlike bobs. "You're one lady who concocts some wild ways to die! Like that poison fish—and in a bubble bath, too. After I read that chapter, I put away all my bath products except for the oils. Oils would kill something like that, wouldn't they?"

"The arsenic in the toothpaste—that was the best," April declared. "I thought Maxie was never going to figure that one out. And when the murderer slipped a tube into her bathroom and she almost brushed her teeth with it, I practically died!

"And stop that infernal bobbing, Teri. I think you exercise just to annoy me." April patted her rounded stomach. She was in the fifth month of her second pregnancy and already over her weight-gain limit.

Teri drew her head up from her knees and folded herself into a round ball up against the foot of the sofa. "Sorry." She threw a contrite look at April. At twenty-four, Teri saw motherhood as some distant, mystical experience—to be revered but experienced in some other lifetime.

Jennifer looked at the three women and tried to decide if they were dedicated writers or eccentric twenty-somethings who had somehow got lost in the space-time continuum.

Monique cleared her throat, and everybody turned toward the maple rocking chair that served as her throne.

"Jennifer has come to us with a plotting problem. She's not writing to please you or to come up with yet another clever way to bump off her latest victim. She is trying to devise a plot that will sell, and personally, I think a gun might have more appeal than poison fish or toothpaste. Tell us what you have in mind, Jennifer. It's refreshing that you're soliciting advice in the outline stage for once—before you've set Maxie off on some . . . unique adventure."

Jennifer didn't exactly hate Monique, but a plot about a dead, one-book, holier-than-thou author was involuntarily forming in her mind.

"Say a man decides to kill a woman," Jennifer said aloud, "and he decides to use a gun."

"But a gun?" Teri whined. "Get real, Jen." Her body was now twisted into something resembling one of the pretzels Leigh Ann continued to eat.

"You use guns all the time in your books, Teri," Jennifer reminded her. "In that chapter you read us last week, Yasmine Simone had a gun secreted in that ruffled eyelet pillow on her bed."

"That's because I write romantic suspense, and my characters have to be prepared. Besides, guns are *sex*-y. Don't let anybody tell you any different."

"I'll say," April murmured. "When Yasmine and her man even think about danger, they hop into the sack."

"Sex is life-affirming." Leigh Ann sighed between bites. "But you haven't answered Teri's question, Jen."

"A gun is easier to control than a knife, less risky than poison, and less messy than explosives."

"But you're in control of the story," April insisted. "When Whacky the Duck wandered into that construction site that Mama Duck had told him to stay away from, I knew he'd be all right because I wrote in Barkley the Dog to protect him. *We're* the creators, Jen. We control what happens in our plots. And pass me those damn pretzels."

Leigh Ann scooped up the bowl and took it to April, setting it on top of her rounded stomach. "If you'd let that duck get eaten by Johnny the Junkyard Dog, kids would learn to listen to their mothers."

An exasperated intake of air from the direction of the rocker silenced the group. Leigh Ann quietly took her place on the sofa.

"You were saying, Jennifer?" Monique said.

"I want to write something more reality-based, something that might even happen. That poison toothpaste stuff doesn't occur in real life, product tampering aside."

"Give us a scenario," Monique ordered.

"Say the victim is an influential businesswoman living in one of those plush, high-rise, security buildings in Atlanta. You know, the kind with a doorman—the works."

"First your murderer's got to get past the muscle," Teri declared.

Monique threw her a withering stare.

"No problem. He can pose as a deliveryman with a basket of fruit," Leigh Ann suggested.

"What if they won't let the murderer take it up to her door?" Jennifer asked. "Some places won't, you know."

"A fumigator—how about that?" Teri threw in.

"The doorman would call the tenant and maybe the extermination company to check."

"Insurance."

"What are you babbling about now?" Leigh Ann asked April.

"It's simple. With so many lawsuits going on these days, all the murderer has to do is pretend to be an insurance investigator. He convinces the building staff that he wants access to an upstairs window—maybe in a stairwell or an empty apartment—while he observes the building across the street," April explained. "The building where some jerk works or lives. The murderer says he wants to catch on film this creep who says his back is hurt or he can't walk doing some kind of strenuous activity."

"Only he's not really watching for some person defrauding the insurance company," Jennifer said.

"No way, girl!" Teri exclaimed. "He's spending his

time casing the place and figuring out how to get into this woman's apartment."

"And the doorman becomes familiar with this person to the point he lets him come and go without suspicion," Leigh Ann added.

"But he does it in disguise—wig, facial hair, bulky clothes, whatever," Teri suggested.

April supplied the finishing touch: "And he watches the victim's apartment until he knows the woman's habits and finds a way to slip in and do the deed."

"That might work," Jennifer declared. A tingle began in her toes and crept unwillingly up her whole body. She'd have to wait until a week from Wednesday to make her trip to Atlanta. (Dee Dee had scheduled a baby shower and two wedding rehearsal dinners in the interim.) But she could wait, especially now that she knew just how she would gain admittance to Penney Richmond's apartment building.

Chapter 6

The most lavish dinner on earth would hardly be compensation for suffering through a Friday evening with some guy she barely knew asking questions like "What was your major?" or "What kind of music do you like?" and "How do you make those vegetables into those flowers?"

Jennifer looked at her watch. Seven forty-five. Mr. Sam Culpepper was already fifteen minutes late. Maybe she'd be lucky and he wouldn't show.

Jennifer hated dating. Once she'd threatened to copy an eight-by-ten sheet with answers to the twenty most boring date questions and hand it out at her front door before a man even got his foot across her threshold. Why did a guy need to know her favorite color on a first date? Was he going to buy her a Jag or order new furniture for her living room? Besides, her color preference changed day to day, and, when she was in a particularly ugly mood, hour to hour.

She sighed and dabbed at her cheek with a brush covered with peach blush as she looked at her face in the bathroom mirror. Her hair was pulled up in a French twist and her bangs bowed becomingly over her forehead. Two wispy curls draped the sides of her face.

25

She tugged at the side of her black sheath dress. She was losing weight again, and she needed every ounce. Her almost nonexistent curves were disappearing, and she couldn't afford another wardrobe in a smaller size. It happened every time she got caught up in writing a book. She'd forget to eat—and sometimes to sleep—coming abruptly out of her creative stupor to find the clock reading three A.M.

Why had she agreed to go out with this guy, anyway? She had no interest in him whatsoever. She could tell that easily enough from their encounter at the reception. He was brash, presumptuous, impertinent—in short, abhorrent.

Well, no problem. She'd give him one hellish date, and then she'd never hear from him again. It was easier than letting him become infatuated with his self-created image of her and having to wade through flowers and chocolates and love notes begging her to have his child.

Sorry, Jaimie. This one wasn't daddy material. She'd know it when *he* came along. In her novels she had frequently recounted the unmistakable signs of true love—even with her heroine up to her hips in corpses. In her books, the heroes always knew just what to do, to say, to—

The doorbell sounded. She checked her mascara one last time, brushed away a wayward lash, grabbed up her bag and shawl, and rushed to the front door.

She threw it open and there stood . . . an eight-year-old boy wearing a striped T-shirt and jeans, holding one long-stemmed white rose. "This man . . . this man, he gave me some money and asked me to, um, he asked me to come up here and ring your bell." His voice rose at the end of the sentence as though asking a question.

"Yes," Jennifer said impatiently.

"This man . . . this man wanted you to . . ."

Jennifer swallowed all the words that were trying to crawl out of her mouth. "Exactly where *is* this man?" she asked as calmly as she could.

"This man . . . he was downstairs . . . in his car . . . in front of our building. . . ."

She snatched the rose from the child's hand and tossed it inside the door. "Thank you," she said through clenched teeth. If Sam Culpepper thought for one minute that she was going to dash down to his car without his even bothering to climb the stairs . . .

She rummaged in her bag until she unearthed two one-dollar bills. "Here, you take this and you tell 'this man'—"

"You can tell him yourself," Sam said, coming up the hall. "Sorry I'm a few minutes late. No spaces were open in front. Somebody must be having a party. I circled the lot three times, but I still had to park all the way around back. I sent my friend up to let you know I was here, but I'd be a few minutes late. Did he explain?"

Jennifer looked from the boy's grinning face to Sam's and down to the bouquet of white roses he was holding. Was this Sam? He hadn't looked this handsome the day of the wedding. He was taller than she remembered, and his curly dark hair was slicked back with a few sexy stray strands escaping to brush the top of his right eyebrow. And his eyes were a deep, dark blue.

She shook her head. "He was trying to say something, but I wasn't quite sure what."

"Did he give you the rose?"

The rose? Where had she put the damn rose? Oh, that's right, she remembered. "Of course he did. I laid it inside the door so I could look in my purse for a tip." She scooped it up and held it so Sam wouldn't notice the damaged petal that threatened to fall off.

She turned toward the boy. "Thank you . . ."

"My name's . . . my name's . . . Eddie."

"Thank you, Eddie. You can go home now."

"Whoa. Wait just a minute. I borrowed this young fella from his mother, and she made me promise to see him back downstairs. Are you ready?"

Paternalistic. Nice touch. "Yes," she said, clutching her bag and shawl in her right hand, the rose in her left.

"You might want to put these in water before we take off," he suggested, handing her the bouquet.

There was nothing to do but take it. The injured petal fluttered to the floor as the bouquet joined the single flower. She watched it drift down as though in slow motion.

She looked up and grinned sheepishly. "I'll be right out."

She slipped into the narrow space that served as a kitchen and frantically looked about. No one had given her flowers in a long time. All her vases were boxed up in the closet. She grabbed a ceramic teapot, filled it under the faucet, and plopped the roses in.

The man brought you flowers, and he looks gorgeous. Don't get distracted. Remember your mission. You're to get rid of this guy. You're a woman with a plan. And Jaimie, be quiet. That little display of fatherly concern doesn't mean diddly.

When she returned to the front door, Sam was bending down admiring something the boy was clutching in his hand. It looked suspiciously like the flattened carcass of a frog.

"Okay, we're a go," she announced. Now she was sounding like some escapee from flight attendant school.

Sam took her shawl, draped it over her shoulders, and offered her his elbow.

Eddie ran ahead and punched the *down* button on the elevator. He stood swaying back and forth, waiting for them. "She's . . . she's pretty," he said, covered his face, threw back his head, and laughed.

"I noticed that, too," Sam agreed.

Jennifer and Sam dined on the veranda, that is, if a French restaurant can have a veranda. But then, she supposed, all outdoor porches in Georgia, French or otherwise, could be termed verandas.

The stars twinkled in the black of the night. The breeze was unusually warm for so early in spring. The food—well, the food was adequate. What could she say? Dining out is a mixed blessing for a caterer, especially one who worked for a cook as exacting as Dee Dee.

But the wine—the wine was yummy. And deceptive. One glass was normally Jennifer's limit, and she had had two. If Sam had looked gorgeous before, he was looking downright heavenly about now.

"So you're a caterer and you write books on the side. What'd you major in at college that you wound up doing something like that?"

Jennifer almost choked on the sip of wine she was savoring. She coughed and cleared her throat. "Psychology."

"Psychology?"

"Yeah. I like to think of it as one of those freedom majors."

"What do you mean—a *freedom* major?"

"You can't do anything with it, so you're free to do whatever you want."

"Yeah. I got one of those, too—English."

She raised her wineglass in a mock toast.

Sam leaned closer. "I want to ask you something else."

"Blue," she said. "At the moment, it's a deep, dark blue." She stared into his eyes. "But this afternoon it was more of a mauve, and yesterday—"

"What are you talking about?" he asked, taking the wineglass from her hand and setting it next to his, well out of her reach.

She blinked and shook her head. "Ask away."

"When you're catering an event, I suppose you hear a lot of what's going on. How do people react to you?"

"Like furniture. I like to think of myself as a nice, mahogany sideboard—eighteenth-century American."

"Elegant, classic—I can see how . . ." He shook his head. "My God, I'm beginning to understand you."

She smiled. The wine was definitely giving her a warm fuzzy glow. "They either treat me like furniture or they hit on me. But mostly it's furniture. One time at a bar mitzvah some joker was telling his wife about sleeping with her best friend. He'd got her off in a corner, and I swung by with a salver. I heard the whole sorry story while she cried, and I cried, and she stuffed her mouth with cheese straws. The three of us—we could have been in their den at home—with me as the TV tray."

Sam nodded. "Good. When Steve Moore calls you for a catering job, I want you to take it."

She pinched off a piece of warm, crusty bread and popped it into her mouth. The conversation was taking a decidedly unpleasant turn. Jennifer screwed up her face. She sensed some of the aggressiveness she had found so irritating in Sam at the wedding breaking through his perfect-man veneer.

She swallowed. "I don't like him. He's yucky."

"Of course you don't like him, but I'm asking you to do it anyway. Don't worry. I'll be there with you."

"You? Not without a TB test, you won't." She shook the fog she had encouraged from her mind. The flow of the conversation was finally falling into place. Mr. White Roses Sam was attempting to seduce her *into* her catering outfit, not *out of* her intimate apparel. How dare he use her like that?

"What'd he do? Kill somebody?"

"He didn't exactly *do* anything. He wrote a book that could well become a bestseller."

She rolled her eyes. "So who—other than me—hasn't?"

"Do you remember when Kyle Browning committed suicide last fall?"

"Sure. I always liked him when he was on national TV. Then he got mixed up in that scandal when all those news people died in that hurricane in the Carolinas, and he got banished from New York to Macon. And then he jumped off the Channel 14 building like that. . . . It didn't make any sense. The skyscrapers are a lot higher in New York."

"Some of us don't think Browning's death was a suicide, and—"

"And you think Steve Moore knows something. So why don't you just ask him?"

"I did. He's not talking—at least not to me. He insists he doesn't know anything."

"If you think Moore is saving his secrets for his book, then you'll have no story once the book is out. You'll look like one of those tabloid reporters who's out to scoop something Moore is ready to tell anyway." She really should have a clearer mind if she were going to discuss anything more complicated than her list of dreaded date questions. Those she could answer while plotting an entire twenty-page short story.

"But I don't think Moore's book addresses Browning except from the aspect of his so-called suicide. Moore will capitalize on the publicity surrounding Browning's death, but he won't dare speculate on murder."

"Why are you so sure Moore knows something?"

"He has to. They were friends for years, and when Browning came to Macon, Moore worked with the man every day. He may not even realize what he knows."

They sat in silence for several seconds as Sam studied Jennifer's face. "So, what do you say? Will you help?"

Jennifer plucked off another piece of bread, swirled it in the sauce on her plate, and ate it. "Now why in the world would I do that?"

Sam shrugged. "I want to write a book exposing Browning's murder, but there's no way I can collect this information on my own. I need someone undercover, someone not connected with the news media, someone Moore likes—someone like you. I'll pay you—just not right now. Part of the advance and part of the royalties. Once I get a contract—"

Jennifer's head suddenly cleared. "I want my name on the cover—first. I may not have any hard news experience, but I'm lousy with book smarts. I've got eight full-length novels finished, all with a beginning, an end, and no sagging middles—at least, not too saggy—which is more than you've got. If I even breathe on pages that actually go into production, I want credit."

"We'll have to hash out that name thing. I personally think it'd be more fair if we were credited alphabetically."

"I just bet you do, Mr. *Culpepper*."

"We can work out the details later, but for now: have we got ourselves a deal?" Sam offered her his hand across the table.

Jennifer took it and shook it. "I want it in writing."

Sam's book had about as much chance of happening as a snowstorm hitting Macon—and that was only if it turned out that Browning had actually been murdered. Still, Jennifer couldn't resist any opportunity that might put her name on a book cover. She'd go ahead with her plan to kill Penney Richmond, but she'd help Sam, too. She'd consider it multiple submissions, as eggs in different baskets. One way or another, she was going to break into print.

Chapter 7

Dear Ms. Richmond:

It's people like you who give book publishing a bad name. The careless manner with which you treat unpublished writers is inexcusable. You had my manuscript, *The Corpse Found a Home*, for close to a year and then refused it. Just what were you doing with it? Learning how to read?

Too subtle. Jennifer wadded up the sheet of personalized stationery and tossed it at the wastepaper basket next to her desk.

Muffy leaped from a curled position on the floor and batted the paper wad in midair. After knocking it to the floor, she collapsed onto the rug.

Jennifer sighed and stared out the open window that faced the grassy common area of the apartment building. Tulips and jonquils splashed color around the budding trees.

A couple spread out a blanket and settled beneath the shade of a blooming, pink dogwood. A pleasant way to spend a beautiful Sunday afternoon. And a pleasant place for a grave site. Would you like to be buried there, Penney?

Dear Ms. Richmond:
I hate your guts. I wish you were dead.

Not subtle enough. She scrunched the page into a tight ball and sent it off to join its brothers in the growing paper pile.

Muffy yawned widely, whined, and watched the paper as it flew past.

Dear Ms. Richmond:
A disease exists in the literary community, a disease that attacks and cripples the creative forces of young writers. It sucks the life from them, draining them of their talent, their hopes, and their dreams. And you—Penney Richmond—are the virus that causes that disease.

Not too bad. Fairly poetic. And it wouldn't look bad in print. Even if the press didn't quote the entire letter, they couldn't butcher it beyond recognition—or so she hoped.

Jennifer scrawled her name across the bottom and folded the stationery. She slipped it into an envelope, licked the flap, and sealed it. It would go out in Monday morning's mail. She'd need another one for Tuesday and a third, maybe even a fourth. Yes, a fourth. One letter meant irritated; two angry; three irate; but crazy didn't start until at least four.

She pulled out another sheet of paper.

Dear Ms. Richmond:
The sins we commit are tallied.

She squished the sheet into a tiny ball. It was better not to mention sin. Murder, after all, was a biggie.

How was she ever going to create three more convincing letters? She tapped her pen impatiently against the desktop. She hated writing letters . . . but her serial killer in *Poisoned Pen, Poisoned Heart* tormented his victims with vicious notes for weeks before he murdered them.

She went to the hall closet and rummaged through the manuscripts, extracted one, and carried it back to her desk, Muffy close at her heels. Leafing through the printed pages, she stopped at page thirty-seven. There it was, Marcus's first threatening letter. All she had to do was substitute the word *bullet* for *knife*.

I'm sitting in the dark thinking about how I'm going to kill you. The bullet will pierce your heart and stop it suddenly in mid-beat. I will hear that little gulp of air rushing to fill your chest cavity and deflate your lungs like useless, overstretched balloons. And I will silently watch your astonished face as your life gently ebbs from your irreparably damaged body.

Yuck. What kind of demented mind had she been suppressing? No matter. The letter would do just fine. No sane person would write something like that.

She copied it in pen onto a blank sheet of paper. She didn't need to sign this one. The first letter would provide a sample of her handwriting.

All she had to do was find two more letters. That would be a cinch. Her villain, nasty creature that he was, had written at least eight. She was on her way. Once all the letters had been sent, they'd lay the perfect trail for the police to follow when Penney Richmond turned up dead.

Chapter 8

" 'I've never met anyone like you," he whispered. His greedy mouth found hers as he crushed her to him, leaving her breathless. His fingers kneaded the silky flesh of her neck and then fell to explore the sensual secrets of her body. He groaned.' "

"He's not the only one groaning, Leigh Ann," Jennifer muttered from her spot on the floor next to Monique's sofa.

"You're not supposed to interrupt." Leigh Ann's eyes flared as she stuck out her diminutive chin. "You just don't like love scenes."

"Oh, no, sweetie. You don't get off that easy, Leigh," Teri said. "You've spent two hundred pages throwing these two people together and pulling them apart and all your hero can think of to say is 'I never met anyone like you'? He's met dozens of women like her, but he never got one quite as pure as she is into his bed. She makes his blood boil. Honey, let us see him *sim*-mer." Teri's shoulders undulated with each syllable.

"So what do you want him to say? 'Hey, babe, you make my blood boil'?"

"Nice alliteration," April observed.

"Is that the best you can say about my writing?"

"It wasn't your writing. The boiling blood was my idea," Teri reminded her.

"Ladies, please." Monique spoke in a quiet, commanding tone. "You know the rules, Jennifer. When one group member is reading her work, we all listen. No comments are welcome until she has finished. Do we all understand? Go on, Leigh Ann. I think you were somewhere amid the sensual secrets of your heroine's body."

" 'Sensations he had never experienced stung his fingertips as he . . .' "

Maybe Leigh Ann was right, Jennifer thought. Maybe she had no romance left in her. She'd given Sam a chance Friday night, and look what he'd done with it. He'd only asked her out to gain access to Steve Moore, and she'd let him seduce her into agreeing. He hadn't even done it with sex. He'd found her Achilles' heel—the lure of writing a true-life crime book.

She hoped she hadn't made a complete fool of herself when he took her home. He'd walked her to her apartment, and she turned to say good night, leaning back against the door, still warm and comfortable from the wine. He took the key from her hand and moved toward her. She closed her eyes as she felt his breath come close to her face. And then she heard the tumblers click in the lock and the door give way behind her. Her eyes popped open, and he slipped the key in her hand.

"Thanks for the evening. It was fun." He kissed the tip of his index finger and touched it to the end of her nose. "Let me know as soon as Moore books the party. See ya."

He turned, stuffed both hands into his pockets, pulling the back of his jacket unbecomingly apart, and sauntered off toward the elevator.

Men. She hadn't wanted Sam to kiss her, but . . . Oh, hell. She didn't know what she wanted.

" 'Gasping, they parted, her breast heaving with unbridled passion. "You must leave before someone finds you here.' "

"You mean they still didn't *do* it?" Jennifer asked.

"Of course they didn't *do* it! I'm building tension here, Jennifer. I don't know why you can't grasp the simple dynamics of the genre."

"Don't worry about Jennifer, Leigh. When she has two people alone in a room together, only one of them comes out alive," Teri said.

"All right. April, let's start with you," Monique said. "What is your opinion of Leigh Ann's scene?"

"Well, it certainly stirs the senses. I did have one question about logistics. When he's on the floor and she's on the bed, just exactly how were they able to . . ."

Four whole days, and Sam hadn't called her—not that she cared. If it weren't for Jaimie, she'd be happy if she never saw another man. She'd considered having Jaimie through artificial insemination, but she just didn't think it would be fair. She could hear herself trying to answer Jaimie's questions.

"Why don't I have a daddy at home like other kids?"

"Your dad is a famous astronaut. He's on the first manned flight to Mars and won't be back for three years."

"When he gets back, can he come to my birthday party?"

And there would be other questions.

"What's my dad look like?"

"That's hard to say. The records describe him as tall with dark hair slicked back with just a few sexy strands straying loose to brush his right eyebrow. And he had the deepest, darkest, bluest eyes."

She shook her head. Obviously she had too much on her mind, and her anger at Sam was getting mixed up with her thoughts of Jaimie. That little paternalistic display with Eddie the other night at her apartment wasn't helping her keep them separate.

"Jennifer?"

"What?" she asked.

"What did you think of Leigh Ann's scene?" Monique repeated.

Curses. She didn't have a clue how the hero had almost seduced the heroine this time. "It was great . . . great and unique."

"Did you really think so?" Leigh Ann gushed. "Everyone else trashed it so badly, but if you thought it was good—"

"Maybe *good* is too strong a word. It could use some work. I agree with what Teri said."

"Teri? Teri told me to start over. What's with you?" Leigh Ann demanded.

"Are you all right, Jennifer?" Monique asked in the maternal tone that drove everyone mad.

"I'm fine. I'm just a little ambivalent about Leigh Ann's scene."

"Maybe we should let this drop until Leigh works on it and brings in a revision next week. Did you have something for us to discuss?" Monique asked, staring straight at Jennifer.

"Yes. I need a perfect alibi—for my murderer. I need to establish beyond a doubt that he was somewhere else when he committed the crime."

"Oh, one of those Columbo-type cases that no one can

crack because nobody has a clue who did it," April gushed. "I just love those. They go so well with peanuts. What's in that bowl over there, Leigh Ann? I hardly had time for supper before I came over."

Leigh Ann scooped up the dish of Christmas-striped hard candy and presented it to April with a flourish.

"That baby is going to be addicted to sugar and salt before it even gets out of the womb," Teri declared, rolling onto the floor, grabbing her ankle and pulling her calf up against the back of her thigh.

April dropped the piece of peppermint back into the bowl and set it down on the end table.

"Just where were we last time we discussed this plot?" Monique asked.

Leigh Ann sucked hard on a piece of candy. "I remember. We had the murderer masquerading as an insurance investigator in the victim's fancy apartment building."

"Right, but forget that," Jennifer said. "What I need now is an alibi that the murderer has set up for the night of the crime."

"What if you have him attend a society party in his honor, and have him slip out in the middle of it and back in again?" April suggested. "That's worked in lots of plots. No one ever knows what time it is at those galas."

"No. There aren't any galas to go to."

April clucked her tongue. "Jennifer, just what is going on with you? You act like you've lost all control over your story."

A bead of sweat formed on Jennifer's forehead. "It's just that . . . my murderer . . . is a recluse, and his character is essential to the plot."

"He can't be a complete recluse," Leigh Ann argued. "Where's the fun in that? I say have him seduce some woman and then knock her out somehow so that when she wakes up in the morning, she's in his arms and swears he's been there all night."

Such a simple solution, and certainly not an original one. She was amazed she hadn't thought of it herself. But it had one major flaw: where would she find a man to seduce?

Chapter 9

A huge, fenced-in dirt lot bathed in Mother Nature's best morning sunlight—that's what was across the street from O'Hara's Tara, Penney Richmond's apartment building. Jennifer stared at it in disbelief. No apartments, no stores, no offices, not even a construction site—just dirt—and a sign proclaiming the COMING SOON of Atlanta's newest professional complex. Well, not soon enough!

What kind of insurance claim was she going to investigate in an abandoned lot, probably the only vacant lot in Atlanta?

"I ain't gonna sit here all day while you survey the landscape," the cabbie growled behind her.

Jennifer fished around in the bottom of the tote bag that held her purse and the video camera she'd borrowed from Dee Dee as part of her cover. Her hand closed on a twenty-dollar bill. She thrust it through the car window and into the hand of the cabbie. He looked at the money and then back at Jennifer. "Some tip! Next time, walk!"

Oh, crumb. Things were not going well. She'd been hoping he'd give her back her two dollars change. Dee Dee was right. The catering business was bringing in barely enough money to live on, and she couldn't make it at all if it weren't for all the cholesterol-laden hors d'oeuvres Dee Dee insisted she take home after every job. She certainly didn't make enough to support a life of crime.

Well, no matter. Steve Moore had called, his beautiful voice oiling through her phone. The date for his party was set for this Saturday, and she had boosted Dee Dee's rates so as not to insult him. Hopefully, she'd clear enough money to do in Penney Richmond.

The cabbie was still glaring at her, waiting for enough of a break to let him get back into the stream of traffic. Her image would be burned into his mind. Well, let it burn. It might be better if he did remember her—a pudgy frump with long dark curly hair and glasses.

She must look ridiculous, but it didn't matter how she looked as long as she didn't look like Jennifer Marsh. She wasn't an expert at disguise like her character Maxie Malone, and she certainly didn't have Maxie's resources. But then this was real life. She had to settle for an outfit she'd found at Goodwill, glasses from Eckerd's Drugs, and a wig her mother had bought her when she played Snow White in her seventh grade class production. Her one fling with fame—but not her last!

She shoved the oversized, brown-rimmed reading glasses back onto the bridge of her nose and stared at the apartment building directly across the street. It came into focus at one and a half times its normal size. What a majestic building—so *big*—and all glass, gold, and steel, with lush potted plants.

Guarding the entrance was a gray-suited, white-gloved doorman. White gloves? Where did he buy them? Through a supply catalogue for doormen? They left such *ordinary* fiber evidence.

She brushed the wiry black curls of her wig off her shoulder and sighed. So here she was in Atlanta on a Wednesday morning, and there, across the street, was the apartment building where Penney Richmond lived. And behind her—behind her was the vacant lot. She'd have to devise some other plan to get into Penney's building.

Jennifer tugged at the towel she'd belted beneath her shapeless dress to provide some girth and pushed the loosely knit sleeves of her mud-colored cardigan up to her skinny elbows. Enough of this dillydallying. It was time to get to work, time to cross the street, time to case the joint.

She joined the crowd as it swept her the fifty feet to the stoplight and the crosswalk. The light turned red. Four cars rushed through the intersection as the little walking man in the crossing light replaced the red hand. He tried to lure her into the street, but she was too savvy for him. She'd been to Atlanta before and she knew better.

Without warning, the crowd surged forward, buoying Jennifer and depositing her on the opposite corner. Whoa! Managing curbs that were one and a half times lower than they appeared was not an easy task. She had to have a moment to steady herself.

Suddenly she felt an overwhelming need for caffeine. She preferred her caffeine in the form of chocolate—lots of chocolate, the dark semisweet kind—but coffee would do in a crunch, and floating in her direction, mixing with the stench of gasoline, was the unmistakable aroma of coffee laced with vanilla and almonds. She sniffed the air. The odor seemed to be wafting from an establishment directly in front of her.

Jennifer tugged open the heavy wooden door of the

café and slipped inside. A woman in a long, loose-fitting floral dress was filling honey jars behind a counter. Jennifer settled herself onto one of the bar stools. The woman shoved the jar aside and licked her index finger before wiping her hands on a towel.

"What'll you have?" she asked. "We've got some wonderful herbal teas," she suggested, eyeing the bulge under Jennifer's dress.

Jennifer looked down at the roundness the towel was creating. "Oh, no, I'm not . . . Just make it coffee—strong coffee with lots of caffeine and some kind of chocolate flavor if you've got it."

What rotten luck! She'd tried to leave all thoughts of Jaimie at home. She didn't want him/her/whatever mixed up in this mess with Penney Richmond.

"Mint is the day's chocolate flavor," the woman explained. "Will that do?"

"Just fine."

The woman plopped a large mug of fragrant coffee in front of her. "Honey and cream are right in front of you. That'll be a buck fifty."

Jennifer handed her the money and carried her cup to a small window table where she could watch the crowds as they walked down Penney Richmond's street. Jolene Arizona would have no trouble getting into that apartment building. Jolene would sleep with the doorman. But then Jolene slept with everybody. What a disgusting thought. After all, she had Jaimie to think of, an example to set for her child-to-be.

What kind of example was murder?

"How far along are you, honey?"

The words seemed to float up from nowhere.

"When are you due?"

Jennifer turned, and in the shadow of a tall, wooden booth she could detect the outline of a tiny, fragile woman. Her face lay in shadow but light streamed through her wispy white hair, creating something like a halo about her head.

"Are you talking to me?" Jennifer asked.

"Of course I'm talking to you. Do you see anyone else in here?" The woman leaned forward, bringing her wrinkled face into the light. "Now bring your coffee over here and sit with me for a spell."

What was she to do? Say "Don't bother me. I'm in the middle of planning a murder"?

She took a big swallow of coffee and carried the cup over to the booth. "I'm sorry, but—"

"Sit."

Jennifer slid onto the heavy brown vinyl.

"Now what do you think you're doing drinking coffee in your condition?"

"My condition? Oh, no. You don't understand. I'm not pregnant. I'm just—"

"It's nothing to be ashamed of these days, child. I see that there's no wedding ring on your finger. It's better to just admit what you've done and get on with your life. Better for both you and the baby. You *are* keeping it?"

Keeping what? The towel? Okay, so her disguise wasn't what she had in mind, but why not go with the flow? If the police came looking for a pregnant woman, it certainly wouldn't be Jennifer Marsh.

"Did your boyfriend leave you?"

"Boyfriend?"

"Your baby's father, dear. Did he leave you? You seem so lost and forlorn."

"No, of course not."

"Then he's standing by you. That's so admirable in today's climate of irresponsibility."

"No, not exactly."

"Oh, my my." The old lady found Jennifer's hand and clasped it firmly in hers. "You can tell Aunt Emmie about it. He didn't have one of those sex changes. . . ."

"He's dead. Dead and gone. Buried. And I don't want to talk about it." Lying was not easy, especially to a tenderhearted old lady who wanted to know her towel had a good future.

Aunt Emmie patted Jennifer's hand.

"Grrrrrrrr."

Jennifer studied Emmie's beatific face. "Did you just growl at me?"

"No, silly. Tiger is jealous." She dropped Jennifer's hand and lifted her large pocketbook from beside her and onto the tabletop. A black nose, two potato-chip ears, and tiny black eyes on a head about the size of an orange popped out of the bag. "Grrrrr." Canine teeth the thickness of toothpicks curled up over a thin upper lip.

Jennifer jerked back. "What in the—"

"Well, I'm not quite sure. I'm fairly certain he's a dog. I found him, you see, on the street near here. I thought he was a pup but that was two years ago."

"And you *kept* him?"

"What was I to do? Leave the poor soul to starve to death?"

Sure. Why not? Any creature that looked like a leftover from a horror movie should not be encouraged, and definitely not fed. She'd seen *Gremlins*.

"I don't know what you should have done, but carrying him around in your purse—"

"Shhhh." Aunt Emmie snapped the purse shut and returned it to the bench as the lady behind the counter approached the booth.

"More tea, Mrs. Walker?"

Mrs. Walker's purse gave an unnatural lurch to the left.

"No thank you, Lori. We're just fine over here." She waved the woman away.

Mrs. Walker reached down and opened her purse so the life-form could breathe.

"They don't like animals in here."

Jennifer didn't like animals in here, either. "It's been very pleasant talking with you, Mrs. Walker . . . and meeting Tiger, but I'm only here for the morning from Macon, and I really must—"

"Must you, dear? I get so little company and I hardly get out anymore, just once a day to come down here for tea and sometimes a biscuit. I'll have to be going soon myself before I get too tired. And I forgot my cane. I'll have to wait until the crowd breaks outside before I venture back to my building by myself, and that could be almost two o'clock."

Jennifer sighed inwardly. She should be thinking about murder—*murder*—not helping some poor old lady back to her apartment building. But she couldn't leave the woman to sit all alone in the dark for another four hours. The woman walked—without her cane—so her apartment couldn't be *that* far away.

"Let me help you home," Jennifer offered.

"Oh, no. I couldn't ask you to do that, sweetie."

"Really, it's no bother, and I'm not on any kind of schedule."

"That would be lovely, child. It's just a few feet away

in that big building in the middle of the block—the one with all the glass and gold, the one with the big potted plants out front."

Chapter 10

If Emmie Walker needed a cane, it was to knock people out of her path. She led the way to O'Hara's Tara, introduced a shy Jennifer as her niece to the doorman, and escorted her to the twelfth floor in a gleaming bronzed elevator.

"And what is your name, dear?" Mrs. Walker asked, briskly opening the door and ushering Jennifer into the parquet foyer of the plush condominium.

A name? She had to come up with a name? Wasn't it enough that she'd donned this ridiculous costume complete with faux pregnancy? She should have realized someone would demand at least a name, even if she'd been able to talk her way out of showing proper identification.

Jennifer stared at the back of the little woman's head. A few dark strands mixed in with the thin, silver-white curls, and all she could think of was Sophia on *The Golden Girls*, Sophia who was much more spry than she sometimes let on and who could easily walk the distance from the coffee shop to her building without so much as a pause to catch her breath.

"Sophia," Jennifer said, following the old lady into the living room. The white carpet was so thick, she felt like she was standing on shifting sand.

"Sophia what?"

"Sophia . . . Sophia McClanahan." Rue McClanahan would have to forgive her, but she seemed to have a *Golden Girls* theme going.

"That's an interesting name, dear. Are you Italian on your mother's side? All that thick, dark hair, I should have guessed."

"That sounds right," Jennifer agreed.

A low rumble emitted from Mrs. Walker's purse. She opened it and let the creature out.

Now that Jennifer could see the beast in its entirety, it looked like a mutated Chihuahua. It flew at her feet and fiercely attached itself to the toe of her shoe.

"He loves leather. He's chewed up everything I have, I'm afraid."

"Maybe it's a mineral deficiency—something left by the tanning process," Jennifer suggested, trying to shake the animal off her foot without seeming too obvious.

"Would you like something to drink?" Mrs. Walker offered. "Perhaps a ginger ale? I don't think there's anything in ginger ale that would threaten our little one."

When had her towel become "our little one"? But then, Mrs. Walker was apparently into adoptions. Jennifer would have to see if she could work that generosity to her advantage.

"Ginger ale would be wonderful." If she could just get the woman out of the living room, she could get that growling demon off her shoe.

"You sit down. I'll be right back."

As soon as Mrs. Walker was out of sight, Jennifer pulled the monster from her toe and flattened its snarling carcass against the floor. She knew how to train dogs, and, assuming Tiger was one, she felt it imperative to establish dominance right away. "Consider me an alpha wolf," she warned the squirming mass. "My territory includes my body, shoes, and clothing. You can have everything else as long as you don't mess with me. Got that?"

Tiger gurgled in Jennifer's paralyzing grip. She took that gurgle as acquiescence and let the critter loose. It scampered away to cower under a game table in the far corner of the room.

Mrs. Walker returned carrying a small tray with two crystal, on-the-rocks glasses sporting a bubbling, champagne-colored liquid. "Mr. Walker did so love ginger ale. I keep it around to remember him by." She sighed and sat down next to Jennifer on the brocade sofa.

"I'm sorry. How long has Mr. Walker been gone?"

"A good ten years, I'm afraid."

Jennifer sipped the liquid. "I'm sure you miss him," she added.

"Only when he's late with the alimony check. That teeny-bopper blonde he ran off with"—Mrs. Walker let out a devilish chuckle—"she didn't know what she was in for." She took a sip of ginger ale. "It's true what they say, you know. The best revenge *is* living well."

"And this *is* living well," Jennifer agreed, surveying the room. It looked like something out of *Southern Living*. The furnishings dripped money, and the entire back wall was floor-to-ceiling windows, creating a backdrop with a postcard view of the city's skyline.

"Do you like it here? What are your neighbors like?" Jennifer asked casually.

"It's quite pleasant. Of course, so many of the residents work. Not too many are home during the day, and I don't go out much at night. And what brings you to Atlanta, Sophie?"

She should have put more thought into this name. "Oh, you know, the usual . . ." Something. The usual something. What the heck brought people to Atlanta?

"Your usual monthly doctor's visit? I should have guessed. But I would have thought you'd have a doctor in Macon. Oh, my my. Don't tell me. It's not a rare condition, is it? Something that might threaten our little one?"

Jennifer drew her lips inside her mouth, clamped down on them and gave a curt little nod of her head. She did better letting Mrs. Walker answer for her than she did by herself.

"You don't want to talk about it, do you?"

Jennifer shook her head vigorously. She certainly didn't. She wanted to talk about Penney Richmond. But she'd settle for the bronzed elephant on Mrs. Walker's bookcase.

"You have such exotic things," Jennifer observed. "That elephant, wherever did you get it?"

Mrs. Walker patted her hand. "You like that, do you? Mr. Hammerstein three doors down brought that to me from India last spring when he was there on vacation. It's not so bad, I guess, but it doesn't quite suit my taste. You see that jade Buddha on the shelf above it?"

Jennifer nodded.

"Mrs. Swimmer brought it to me from Japan. I can't stand the monstrosity, but she pops in at the most unexpected times to check on me, so I have to keep it out."

Jennifer needed to get back on course before she got a grand tour of every gift and bauble in Mrs. Walker's collection. Her eyes lighted on the books filling the bottom two shelves.

"I see you have books," she said stupidly. "Are any of your neighbors in the publishing industry?"

Mrs. Walker regarded her quizzically, as if to say, "Do I look illiterate?" Thank goodness, the woman was far too genteel for that!

"The only tenant I'm aware of that is employed in that business is an incredibly annoying creature." Mrs. Walker sipped her drink while an uncomfortable warmth seemed to surge throughout Jennifer's body.

"What does she do?"

"She's one of those high-powered literary agents—married and divorced more than once. I've heard she has men up to her place. I see her dragging in on Fridays. She's just not as young as she pretends to be—has to rest up for her nights out, or in, if you know what I mean." The old woman gave her a sly wink. "But if they've got enough money, the management looks the other way."

Jennifer shook her head in disapproval. "Does she live on this floor?"

"Next one down."

"Right beneath you, then. No wonder you're annoyed by her entertaining. She must make a lot of noise."

"No, dear, she's over in the other section of the building, number 1129, near Mr. Staunton."

Jennifer suspected this Mr. Staunton served as a kind of wire service for the building.

"These units with the view, the ones with a floor plan like this one, are the more expensive ones. They don't come up for sale very often."

Jennifer glanced at her watch. As much as she'd like to stay and pump Mrs. Walker for more information, she had to get back to Macon. Dee Dee had a job scheduled for seven o'clock. She'd barely have enough time to catch a cab back to the bus depot and make it in time to change and get over to the house.

"I didn't realize it was so late," she said out loud. "I've got to get home." She returned her glass to the tray and stood up.

"Must you, dear?"

"I'm afraid I must," Jennifer assured her, moving toward the foyer.

"And when are you coming back? Wednesdays are good for me. I play bridge on Mondays and Thursdays, and I have painting class on Friday. You could come for lunch. Ernie downstairs knows you as my niece." She lowered her eyes in feigned contrition. "I hope you don't mind that little deception, but it makes it so much easier than trying to explain. They're so particular, you see. I guess they're afraid one of us might usher in a mass murderer."

Jennifer could understand their concerns. They had cause to be concerned. She had Penney Richmond's apartment number, but she still had one major hurdle to overcome—figuring out the security system in these units and how she could defeat it.

"Wednesday will be fine. Shall we say about eleven?"

Chapter 11

Sam had some nerve. The only communication Jennifer had had with him since their date had been a brief message on her answering machine: "Hey, beautiful. Don't forget Steve Moore's party. Call me as soon as you hear from him."

When Sam didn't call her back and Moore booked the party for tonight, she'd been reduced to leaving an answering machine message herself. She'd given him Dee Dee's number. And the cad had done just that—called Dee Dee.

So this was how she got to spend her Saturday night. Working with Sam in the kitchen and dodging Steve Moore in the living room.

She dropped a box of utensils loudly on the inlaid stone floor. Sam was definitely more trouble than he could ever be help, and she suspected he hadn't even bothered to get his TB screening. Why else would he refuse to show her the results?

"The test was negative," Sam insisted, opening a large crate and lifting silver trays onto the hand-tiled kitchen counter.

"I still want to see your arm."

"When the test is negative there is *nothing* to see. I do

have a chicken pox scar in a rather interesting place if you'd like to see that."

She wished she didn't have to see him at all, and she certainly didn't want to get acquainted with his anatomy.

"Tuberculosis is a serious disease," Jennifer grumbled, "and if one of our guests—"

"What are the two of you fussing about?" Dee Dee asked, coming through the back door and dropping a large box on the floor.

"Help me out here, Dee Dee," Sam begged. "Jennifer wants to rip my clothes off right here in the kitchen."

Dee Dee stopped in mid-motion and studied Jennifer.

Jennifer made an unintelligible noise. "I don't think he had his TB test done. He's not willing to show me his arm."

"I offered some alternatives, but she didn't seem too interested," Sam piped in.

"Oh, that. Of course he had it done," Dee Dee said. "He brought me the results. Do you think I'd let him serve if he hadn't? The two of you need to get yourselves together. Mr. Moore has seventy-five guests arriving in less than forty-five minutes and only the three of us to feed them."

Dee Dee pointed to Sam. "You set up the wine and punch station. I want you to man it. I'll show you the portions. Don't worry about the hard stuff. Moore got a bartender for that."

"And you," she said, pointing to Jennifer, "set the stove at 250 degrees to warm the stuffed mushrooms, the ham biscuits, and the sausage rolls. The cold canapés are packed in ice, so they'll be fine until we need them. I'm going to set up the hot food station."

Dee Dee swept out of the room carrying a large chafing dish.

"Where did she learn to bark orders like that?"

"The Marines—as a military brat. Eighteen years at twelve bases. No one goofs off around Dee Dee when she's working. She won't tolerate it."

"And what's your excuse?"

"My excuse for what?"

"For not tolerating anything—and me in particular. I thought we had a nice time the other night."

A nice time. Just the words every girl wants to hear—two weeks after a first date. At least he remembered there had been a date. "It was pleasant enough."

"I don't suppose you would call it a date, more like a business dinner, but I thought we got along pretty well."

Terrific. Now their dinner wasn't even a date. If she'd known that, she would have worn blue jeans. But he was forgetting the roses. Roses made it a date no matter what he said, and she had the dried petals to prove it. She'd saved them—to make potpourri, of course.

She opened her mouth to speak, but Sam beat her to it. "Moore's invited most of the brass from Channel 14— the station manager, the producers and anchors from all the news programs. And one or two of the network bigwigs from New York might even show up."

"I'm surprised the police didn't investigate Browning's death as a murder from the beginning." Jennifer opened the box on the floor, extracted a large baking pan, and began unwrapping it.

Sam cocked his head at her. "Oh, yeah? Why do you say that?"

"He came off the top of the building from the rear and into an employee parking lot in the middle of the day. No one saw it happen, and the police estimate that the body lay there for at least half an hour before someone found it."

Sam grinned at her as he uncorked a bottle of wine to let it breathe. "I know. Browning was used to making big splashes. If he decided to take that dive on his own, he would have made it straight into the stream of downtown traffic—preferably rush hour. After all, the man had been before the cameras most of his adult life. It would have made great footage for the evening news. The networks would have picked it up in a minute."

Jennifer slipped the pan filled with mushrooms into the oven. "So who or what are we looking for?"

"Browning was mixed up in that scandal in North Carolina when he was working for the network. He was down there to 'get the experience' of a major hurricane. Only he left his crew in a beach house to ride out the storm while he ducked out supposedly to get in touch with New York and wound up holed up in a public shelter."

"I remember that." Jennifer clucked her tongue. "The crew didn't make it, and Browning's career died with them. What a waste, and all for some stupid news story."

Sam nodded. "Sometimes we journalists can get a little overzealous."

"Sometimes?" She looked him up and down. What was zealous if not posing as a waiter at some party? She noticed the tuxedo shirt looked better on him than it did on her. She really would have to talk to Dee Dee about new uniforms. "Browning never spoke to the press, if I remember correctly, although they were unmerciful in their criticism of him. He just faded away."

"To reemerge right here in Macon."

"So you think there's more to the scandal, more than a single miscalculation?"

"Browning acted like a scapegoat."

"I don't know. I thought he acted like someone who had goofed big-time and was shamed by what he had done."

"Exactly my point. No apologies. He just stuck his tail between his legs and ran. The man had played the system for years. He knew how to work it, but he didn't even try."

"And that's really the question, isn't it?" Jennifer said. "Why didn't he at least try a defense?"

"Exactly."

"Smacks of a payoff."

"Especially in view of the presumed suicide. If he were murdered . . ."

He was doing it again, suckering her in, pulling her into a web of real-life intrigue. The bastard. "So who do you suspect is involved? Someone who will be in that room tonight?" She nodded in the direction of the den.

"Perhaps. Professional hazard: I suspect everything and everybody."

Just as she suspected. He didn't have a clue about who murdered Browning.

"Someone might recognize you when you serve. You were a guest at the wedding."

"Well . . . not exactly."

"Oh, no. Don't tell me you crashed that wedding. And you ate my canapés. Do you know how much a head it costs for an affair like that?"

"Lighten up. Nobody is going to starve if I have a couple of Dee Dee's ham biscuits." He lifted one toward his mouth, but Jennifer grabbed it from him. He caught her wrist with his other hand and for a moment they stared at each other. He had to feel the electricity that ran up her arm.

Jennifer broke his grip and took up the box of biscuits. "No one eats anything until later. And for you that's much later—as in maybe never."

He groaned. "Why don't you like me, Jennifer?"

"We have a professional relationship."

"And which would that be? Writing partners or eighteenth century mahogany sideboard to twentieth century wine dispenser?"

"I can't believe I agreed to this."

"Oh, you agreed, and whether you like me or not, you're lovin' every minute of it."

Chapter 12

Damn! The woman was obnoxious. Moore had invited the guest from hell.

Jennifer ducked back into the kitchen, dropped the tray on the counter, and covered her ears. If she had to listen to that screechy voice any more she was liable to commit an unpardonable act. The woman was constantly demanding more champagne and hectoring Jennifer to "fix more of those cute little bacon-wrapped wieners, will yah, hon." Jennifer had never encountered someone so bereft of redeeming qualities from the top of her bleached blonde hair to the spike of her teal heels.

She shuddered.

Dee Dee stuck her head in the doorway. "Sam told me to check on you. He said you'd reached a volcanic shade of red—which he insisted was not a particularly unusual color for you—and then you disappeared. Are you all right?"

Jennifer drew herself up. "I'm fine, but I'm finished serving this side of the room. If I have to go outside and come through the French doors to get to the other side, I will."

Dee Dee considered her friend. "The woman in teal."

"From the bow in her hair to the toe of her colored hose."

"I think you ought to reconsider," Dee Dee suggested. "Get to know her."

"Know her? I'd like for her to disappear. She's an escapee from some fairy tale, the evil Grizelda. She probably has tiny tots locked in her basement. Did you notice what a taste she has for pork, and you know what they say about the similarity to human flesh."

"Put all that aside, kiddo. She's a literary agent. Big-time stuff. She might do you some good. Her name's Penney Richmond. Ever heard of her?"

Jennifer froze. Her skin prickled to attention as all the blood drained from the upper part of her body and her knees gave way. She slid into one of the kitchen chairs.

"Did you say Penney Richmond?"

How dare she turn up in the flesh? How dare she *have* flesh? Penney Richmond was a voice on the phone, a signature on a letter, an intended murder victim, yes; but was she actually a living, breathing, human being? Maybe *human* was too strong a term.

"What's she doing here?" Jennifer managed to ask.

"So you've heard of her. She's Steve Moore's agent. She got him a deal you wouldn't believe—we're talking six figures easy—and that's just the advance."

"Nonfiction always brings more than fiction," Jennifer said automatically.

"Well, I'm glad to hear that. Maybe this project you're working on with Sam will pan out. It's good you're considering writing about a real-life crime."

And committing one? Would that require real blood?

"But Sam had better not let on who he is," Dee Dee

went on. "If anyone finds out I let him do this . . . Are you sure you're all right?"

Some of the color was returning to Jennifer's cheeks. "Yes. I just need to sit for a minute. You go back to your station, and I'll get some fresh ham biscuits out of the oven and bring them out."

Jennifer stared after her as Dee Dee disappeared back into the hallway. Penney Richmond was *real*. Real. How could that fact have escaped her before now? But she didn't have time to think about that. She had to return to the living room and start serving again. She had to listen to the conversation for Sam. And she had to see Penney Richmond.

She grabbed two oven mitts and pulled the oversized baking pan from the oven. The ham in the biscuits gave a sizzle as she plucked the appetizers from the pan and arranged them on a fresh salver.

She straightened her bow tie, brushed away the hairs that had escaped from her French twist, took three deep breaths, and threw back her shoulders. She could do this. She could walk into that room and pretend everything was just as it had been five minutes ago. Even if it wasn't.

She shouldered the tray and plunged into the melee.

The room was noisy and crowded, with a generous sprinkling of beautiful people, mostly news anchors and a few other TV personalities.

A cackle broke above the din. Penney was somewhere on the left side of the room. Jennifer thought if she stayed to her right, she could effectively serve most of the guests without coming near the woman. She had to put all thoughts of Penney Richmond out of her head for now.

"This is the best damn food I've ever tasted," a rotund

gentleman declared in a non-Southern accent as he swept two ham biscuits into the palm of one hand.

Jennifer managed a smile. "Welcome to Macon. You must be one of Mr. Moore's New York colleagues."

"Actually, no." The man turned toward a circle of men directly behind her and bumped Jennifer's tray into the back of the man just in front of her.

"Ham biscuit?" she offered sweetly.

The beautiful face of John Allen turned to her. He was even more handsome up close than he'd been with the sun creating a corona about his head on his wedding day.

"I hope you didn't get any of that grease on the back of my jacket!"

"I'm sorry, no, of course not. I never pack the trays to the edge for just that reason." She'd pack them any way he liked. She'd stack them up or down, dance around him with a biscuit in each hand, feed them to him personally. Those wonderful chiseled features—the guy had to have great genes. Jaimie could use a few of those genes.

"What's the calorie count?" he asked, a deep furrow forming between his generous eyebrows. "Are they worth it?" he asked seriously.

Jennifer blinked. She'd hoped for something more personal. "I don't know about the ham—I don't eat meat— but the biscuits are the best in Georgia, and the ham is almost fat free."

He offered a mocking half smile. "You one of those nature freaks?" he asked as he bit off a third of the biscuit and then grabbed up a second.

He was considerably more appealing when he didn't talk, but then, she found men frequently were, especially those who had trouble understanding her aversion to animal flesh. They did, after all, seem to *crave* it.

"No." She smiled sweetly. "I just have other preferences."

"Yeah." He turned back to his companion. "You ought to try these biscuits, Lily." Lily, his wife and the first runner-up for Miss Georgia. *She* looked better from a distance.

Lily wrestled the second biscuit from his hand and dropped it back onto the tray. "I don't know how you can eat like that. The worst thing that could happen would be for you to pork up to three hundred pounds again. And be careful of the gristle. You could loosen one of your caps."

Okay, so maybe his genes weren't so great. On closer inspection that chiseled nose looked a tad too chiseled. But whatever his surgeon had to work with originally, he sure turned out one beautiful product.

"People are standing in line for your job. If you lose some hair, I can take care of it, but gain some weight . . . All someone needs is an excuse. Look at what happened to Kyle Browning."

"That's not why they let him go," John insisted. "People died, and Steve says since Kyle survived, he had to be held responsible. Kyle was just doing his job. And Steve says Kyle's job was to move on when the time was right."

Lily's eyes grew dangerously narrow. "I wasn't talking about his weight, you nitwit. I knew Kyle Browning as well as anyone in Macon so don't go telling me what Steve said. And I don't think Kyle was finished with national TV. He was laying low, biding his time, but he had a plan. You, on the other hand, can't seem to see past your next Twinkie. You'll never make it into the big leagues if you don't stop stuffing your mouth."

"Hell, Lily, I hate it when you start in on me like this."

"*You* hate it . . ."

Suddenly, as though in tandem, Lily's and John's eyes turned to Jennifer.

Her cloak of invisibility had suddenly dissolved. She put on her best I'm-dumb-as-a-post-and-didn't-follow-a-word-you-said look. "Another ham biscuit?" she offered.

Lily gave her a drop-dead look, threaded her arm through John's, and pulled him into the crowd.

So Sam was right. Kyle Browning wasn't despondent, at least not according to Lily Dawber, and *there* was a woman who could make any man despondent.

But she would have to consider Kyle's state of mind later. Right now she had a ham biscuit to dispose of. She plucked it from the tray and wrapped it in a napkin. She'd put it in her pocket, but she still had grease stains where she'd once stashed a stuffed mushroom that had fallen on the floor.

She scanned the room—typical party, not a trash can to be seen. Sam would have one behind the bar. She swept in that direction, serving over half of the tray as she made her way across the room.

Sam was practically drooling over a gorgeous brunette as he handed the woman a glass of white wine. Jennifer came up behind him and let the biscuit thunk loudly into the metal can. She set the tray on the counter.

"Find out anything interesting?" Sam asked under his breath.

That Penney Richmond had corporeal form, but then Sam wouldn't be interested in that.

"Yeah, a little. It seems Lily Dawber had more than a

passing acquaintance with Kyle Browning—and he wasn't depressed."

"Anything else?"

Jennifer shook her head. "I was doing great until they noticed I was alive. How about you?"

He wiped his hand on a towel and turned to her. "Bits and pieces. I just wish I knew what any of it meant. New York pretty much dissed the party, but most of Macon's media showed. The consensus seems to be that Moore is exploiting Browning's death to push his book—no big revelation. But I did hear something else that could turn out to be nothing or something big. See that woman over there?"

Even in that crowd, Penney Richmond stood out, and Sam was pointing straight at her. "Someone is threatening to kill her."

Chapter 13

For a moment the room spun. Jennifer grabbed hold of the bar and steadied herself.

"Are you all right?" Sam asked.

"Just fine," she lied.

Sam looked at her keenly. "You didn't threaten that woman, did you?"

She had, but she hadn't meant it. Really she hadn't. Still, she felt branded by her own malicious thoughts. She could almost feel the words *murderer-in-training* glowing in neon across her forehead. Could people just look at her and tell what evil plans she harbored? Surely not. If it were that easy, the world wouldn't need Perry Mason or Sherlock Holmes. But this man Sam—what was it he'd said to her the first time she met him?— reading people was his business.

"I mean, I could tell she was getting on your nerves," Sam continued. "She's loud enough she could be heard in Atlanta, but I never saw your teeth move through that sardonic grin of yours."

Thank goodness! He wasn't as good at reading people as he thought. He'd been wrong about her wanting to go out on a date with him—business meeting or whatever the heck it was—and he was wrong about her threatening

Penney Richmond. That is, wrong about it being tonight, verbally, in this room.

"I didn't utter a word," Jennifer insisted. "I don't threaten guests—at least, not as a rule—and I certainly didn't say anything to her." Nevertheless, sweat was beginning to drip down the back of her neck. She'd done it now, sending out threatening letters without once realizing they'd connect up with a living human being. And now she'd have to pay for it. The whole world would know because Penney was going to tell them.

"Just what did she say?" Jennifer asked as casually as she could manage. "Did she mention any names?"

"No names. Somebody has been sending her letters talking about how they want her dead."

Not dead, really. More like not alive.

"And this is unusual for her?" Jennifer croaked out.

"Not particularly. What is unusual is the frequency and the number. She's had nine in the past week."

Nine? The woman couldn't even count. Jennifer had sent four little letters, hardly more than notes and not *all* of them all *that* unfriendly. She'd been venting, that's all. Where was the harm in that?

A man in a dark suit came up to the bar and asked for two glasses of red wine. Sam poured them and handed them to him. As soon as he was out of earshot, Jennifer leaned across the bar and whispered, "Who does she think is sending her these letters?"

"Some no-talent, wannabe writer."

Jennifer exhaled deeply, like a steam pipe opening to relieve pressure. It was all coming back to her—why she'd decided to murder Penney Richmond in the first place. "Are those her words or yours?"

"Hers. Why?"

"Just curious." Mentally, she added, *and the difference between whether or not I ever speak to you again.*

"My my my." A smooth, deep, male voice spoke near her right ear. "Is my little Jennifer taking a break?" The smell of whiskey wrapped around her head like a scarf.

Jennifer turned to find herself nose-to-nose with Steve Moore.

"I've been looking for you. I know you've been around because most of my guests have been raving about the food, but somehow I managed to miss you all evening."

Miss her? She'd carefully missed him, keeping always to his back. And now she'd made the mistake of staying in one place too long. The old seducer had snared her.

Sam threw her a sly grin and an almost imperceptible nod of his chin. What did he expect her to do? Offer herself up to this lech to get a story for him? She should ram both of their heads together, but instead she smiled. "Mr. Moore. So nice to see you again."

Moore captured her hand between his own soft, fleshy ones. "The pleasure, my dear, is all mine." He bent and brushed the back of her hand with his lips.

"You *must* be starved!" she declared, extracting her hand, grabbing up the almost empty tray off the counter and forcing it between them. "Canapé?"

Moore chuckled. "I can't decide if you're a vixen or a virgin."

"Actually—"

"Dee Dee's looking for you," Sam intervened. "I really hate to interrupt, but if Miss Marsh wants to keep her job, she'd better get back in the kitchen and load her salver with some more food. We wouldn't want her to get fired, would we?"

"Do you type?" Moore asked.

"Type?"

"Type as in keyboard. If you lose your job or if you'd like to do something more interesting with your life, I might be able to find you a place at my office. We're always looking for fresh faces. . . ."

"No, I don't type."

"Now, don't be modest, Jennifer. She's an excellent typist—over seventy words per minute," Sam declared.

"You don't say." Moore dug in his coat pocket and came up with a business card. "Give me a call early Monday morning and we'll see what we can work out." He squeezed her upper arm. "Monday morning," he repeated and turned to join the crowd.

Jennifer shuddered—from rage or revulsion, she wasn't sure which.

"This is great!" Sam said. "Moore's offering you access to the crime scene *and* all the principals involved at the office."

"Yeah, just great." She grabbed him by the ears and drew his face down to hers. "I am *not* throwing myself out as bait to some alcoholic—"

"It's no wonder Moore is so infatuated with you."

Her next thought was to bite off his nose then and there, but instead she just sputtered unintelligibly and let go of his ears.

"Here's how we'll work it," Sam explained. "As far as anyone is concerned, I'm your boyfriend. I take you *to* work; I bring you home *from* work; and I insist on having lunch with you—every day. That way Moore shouldn't have the opportunity to put any moves on you, at least not any serious ones. It shouldn't take you more than a few days to find out what we need to know. I'll be there every step of the way. What do you say?"

She stared into those deep, dark blue eyes not more than a few inches from her own and thought for a moment. If she and Sam were ever going to find out what happened to Kyle Browning, this would be the easiest way. And surely a day or two at Moore's office couldn't be that bad.

"Oh, all right, but I have to have Wednesday off. I have an obligation that day."

"Fine, whatever you say."

Sam suddenly cocked his head, caught the back of her head in his hands, and drew her mouth to his, kissing her gently. She felt an unfamiliar rush tingle through her body. It'd been a long time since anyone kissed her like that.

Sam straightened and retreated beyond arm's reach.

She stared at him open-mouthed.

He shrugged. "If I'm going to play your boyfriend, I need to get into the part."

But did *she* need to get into the part? Somewhere deep down inside her she heard an annoying voice calling to her, the voice of an unborn child who was getting impatient for a father.

A couple had come up to the bar and were motioning to Sam with their empty glasses. Sam turned to help them.

She should have slapped him, but he was counting on her not wanting to make a scene. Well, she didn't have any intentions of making a scene, and if he was interested in her, that was just fine. But Jaimie had better get Sam's role straight right away, and it had *nothing* to do with fatherhood.

Chapter 14

Penney Richmond's disembodied face loomed in front of Jennifer in the dark—all too human, all too *real*. Except for that teal eye shadow—that was pretty fake. And so was that platinum hair. Not to mention those eyelashes.

Jennifer sat up in bed and threw back her hair. Sweat had made her clammy. What kind of murder had she thought she'd been planning? Had she really believed she could kill someone without ever coming into contact with the victim? Penney Richmond was no fictional character to be deleted with a keystroke.

She turned to her nightstand and found her alarm clock. It read two o'clock.

Muffy, dozing on the floor, gave out a gentle *woof* and scratched at the carpeting before settling down again. Who knows what prey she was chasing in her dreams?

Jennifer's prey was chasing her. She hadn't been able to sleep since coming home from the party. How could she? Writing about murder was one matter. Actually depriving another person of her life was quite another, even if that person was a despicable, no-good, lowlife meanie who had no time or compassion for dedicated, talented writers whose only dream was to see their stories in print.

There was no way she could kill this woman for murdering her dreams or for fame or fortune or anything. She couldn't kill spiders, as much as she hated them (most likely a throwback to that Buddhist phase she went through in college). She couldn't even eat meat, for Heaven's sake.

She didn't even *want* to kill her. After all these nightmarish images, she wanted Penney to live forever.

What had she been thinking? Had she lost her mind?

Apparently.

Jennifer slumped back down on the bed, tears gathering in her eyes. Her hand found the flat of her stomach. "Oh, Jaimie," she whispered. "What kind of mother would I be to you if . . . I would never, never hurt anyone, really I wouldn't, no matter how much they deserved it."

Thank goodness Jaimie didn't have ears yet—two sets of chromosomes were needed for that. She/He didn't know, would never know what horrible thoughts her/his mother was capable of. Jennifer would do better. She promised.

She was all done with murder, except the fictional kind, of course. After all, that's what she wrote about. Puzzles. Mind games. Who did what to whom and why. Nothing gritty, nothing gory. She didn't even describe the crime scenes. Too much blood.

Jennifer sat straight up. Of course! That's why her books hadn't sold. That's what Penney Richmond had been trying to tell her in that awful phone call. She had to get down to the nitty-gritty. How could she expect to write effective murder mysteries when she had no clue what murder was all about, knew nothing about how murderers feel?

She couldn't actually harm Penney Richmond, but she

could go through with her plan. She'd simply omit that annoying murder part. She'd walk through her plot down to the very last detail, establishing an alibi, and somehow gaining access to Penney Richmond's home. At last she would know how a killer thinks. And she'd be able to write it, to bring stark reality to her work, to find that missing element. At last she would find success.

And no one would ever know how she'd done it, not even Sam, who was destined to play a part in all this. It had to be that way.

Jennifer settled back against her pillow. Everything was going to be just fine. She and Sam would find out what happened to Kyle Browning, and she would finally discover that secret that her books had been lacking. She could do it. She *would* do it. And Penney would be just fine. Everything would be just fine. She patted her tummy. Just fine.

Chapter 15

"Mr. Moore said I was to call this number first thing this morning."

"Look, whatever your name is—"

"Jennifer Marsh."

"Look, Ms. Marsh, you're going to have to go through Human Resources no matter what Mr. Moore told you. You'll have to put in an application, take a typing test, supply references—the whole shebang. That office is open Monday through Friday from . . ."

Suddenly Jennifer felt a surge of power, power fueled by anonymity and by the knowledge that she had nothing to lose. This was Sam's investigation. She was only along for the ride—and a publishing credit. Of course, her power was tempered by the fact that the phone line could go dead at any minute if the person on the other end of the line caught on and decided to take control of the situation. The trick was to attack so quickly that the woman would never consider hanging up. After all, Jolene Arizona would never allow herself to be pushed around, particularly not when she held a power card: the boss's infatuation with her.

"Is Moore in the office?"

"He is, but he's busy."

"Tell him I'm on the phone."

"I'm afraid you don't—"

"Tell him, or once I get in that office—and believe me, I *will* be working there—we may have to review the status of *all* of the employees. *All!* Have I made myself clear?"

"Just a moment, please."

Jennifer thought she detected a note of amusement in the woman's voice, but most likely it was her imagination. This telephone stuff was actually pretty easy. As long as she didn't die of embarrassment when she finally met the secretary face-to-face, she might even be able to carry it off.

She'd simply have to imagine going into that office the way Maxie Malone would. She would be playing a part, the part of a fearless undercover detective investigating a brutal murder made to look like suicide.

"Jennifer," Moore purred.

How could he make her name sound almost obscene? She might have to change it after this was all over.

"I'm so glad you called. Don't worry about all that red tape Edith was telling you about. After we lost Kyle Browning, the administrative assistant he and I shared quit. We need someone to replace her. We've had temps filling in ever since. I'll take care of everything. Could you start Tuesday morning, let's say about nine o'clock?"

She was a detective investigating a crime. She *had* to keep telling herself that. She was not being thrown into the Roman Colosseum; she was *not*. But she had never felt more Christian in her entire life.

* * *

"You want to know how to seduce someone? Just what *are* you planning?" Leigh Ann asked, her small, dark-haired head peeking up from among the deep cushions of Monique's sofa.

Jennifer had known this was a bad idea as soon as she opened her mouth, but it was too late. She'd asked the question from her rigid perch on Monique's other sofa, and now she'd have to live with the group's response.

"Oooo-eeee, you go, girl!" Teri declared from her place on the floor, one bronzed leg stretched out behind her, the other straight in front.

As much as Jennifer liked Teri, she had always hated people who could do the splits. It seemed unnatural. Teri reminded her of one of her Barbie dolls, the one with the broken leg that swung loosely all the way up to the back of her head.

Teri grinned up at her, bringing her back leg around front and then pulling her forehead down to her knees. "I knew we'd get you sooner or later. I knew we'd draw you into the fold. So what's this new book about anyway?"

"I thought I'd try something in the romance field. I understand that market may be easier to break into."

Leigh Ann threw her an icy stare. "Are you implying something about the quality of my work?"

Leigh Ann had been writing almost as long as she had and still wasn't published. Writers. Why did they all have such fragile egos?

"Look. We don't have to discuss this. As a matter of fact, I'd just as soon we didn't."

For several moments no one said a word, and the creak

of Monique's rocking chair was getting on Jennifer's nerves. Creak. Creak. Creak.

Disagreements were few in this small group of writer-friends, but they were inevitable. All had aspirations, and all felt the system had failed them in some way. But Jennifer was determined to break out of the endless cycle of queries, rejections, disappointment. . . .

Monique's rocker stopped. This was not a good sign.

"Jennifer, what have I said to you more than once? What is the key to success?"

Jennifer searched her mind like an eleven-year-old trying to dredge up the proper answer for the teacher, knowing that whatever answer she gave, the teacher would look at her condescendingly and then correct her. If she waited long enough, the teacher always supplied the answer. And sure enough, she did.

"Inventory. Do you remember my telling you that?"

Jennifer nodded her head.

"And that's what you're working on, isn't it?"

Again Jennifer nodded.

"And what's the important part of inventory?"

She'd gone to Hell, and Hell was being stuck in fifth grade forever with Monique as her teacher.

Monique was nodding, waiting for a response.

"Could you make this a multiple choice question?" Jennifer asked.

Monique ignored Jennifer and shifted her gaze to the others in the room. "Diversification," she stated. "The more fields we try, the more styles we try, the better chance we all have of publishing."

Of course, Monique was right. She almost always was, but Jennifer didn't have to admit it. Monique wasn't even really Monique. She was Betty. Just plain old Betty. She had published one science fiction novel as Monique Dupree, and she'd been Monique ever since.

Jennifer wanted to shout out, "All right, Betty. You made your point, the point I was making when I came in this evening and asked for some help with an idea for a romance novel." But, of course, she never had any intention of writing that romance novel. She really did want to know how to seduce a man. She needed an alibi, and her social life was in such shambles, she hardly remembered how to date, let alone seduce.

"If you want to try something different, why don't you do a picture book for preschoolers?" April suggested.

Images were forming in Jennifer's mind. Writers were always told to write about what they know. She could do one based on the game of Clue. This is a rope, this is a lead pipe, this is a knife, this is Miss Scarlet dead in the library.

Teri was shaking her head forcefully. "No way. Our gal's too much of a plotter. She'd never be happy with that."

"And I suppose by that you mean my Whacky the Duck stories have no plot?"

"No plot?" Teri said. "No plot? Of course not. Your stories are teeming with plot. We never know what dangers are lurking out in the big bad world for that little ducky. I'd like to see him run into a biker gang of Canadian geese and see how you get him out of that one."

"Seduction, guys, please. Seduction—that was the topic of conversation, and I, for one, would like to get back to it," Leigh Ann purred.

Of course she would. Her books breathed seduction.

Jennifer wondered why she was putting herself through this. She should have gone to the bookstore and bought a dozen or so romances and been done with it.

"How old?" Leigh Ann asked Jennifer, sitting up from her envelope of pillows and leaning forward.

"I beg your pardon?"

"How old are the hero and heroine? It makes a difference, you know. Different generations have different patterns. You wouldn't seduce a fifty-year-old man the same way you would a twenty-year-old."

Mentally, Jennifer sighed. Seduction was going to be more complicated than she thought.

"I'm making her late twenties, no more than thirty. And I guess he's something like thirty-two, thirty-three."

"Wonderful ages. Old enough to be sophisticated without being dated. Innovative, but dignified. Trendy, but chic . . ."

"Ethnic group?" Teri asked.

"Does it matter?" Jennifer said.

"Hey, girl, what planet are you from? Of course it matters, Miss White Bread."

"White, American born. This is going to be hard enough to do without adding factors I know next to nothing about."

"Do the flowers, wine, and food scenario," Teri suggested.

"Not a good idea," April countered, patting her belly. "That's how my little number two got started."

"Which is precisely the point," Leigh Ann said. "Who's seducing whom?"

"She, him," Jennifer answered.

"Easiest way," Leigh Ann said. "Okay. She calls him

up and invites him over for dinner. She has fresh flowers on the coffee table, fresh flowers on the dining room table—cut, mixed, no roses. Soft lights—pink bulbs are best; soft music—preferably instrumental; wine but not champagne—never champagne—too obvious. A simple meal—probably pasta, no garlic—with a sinfully rich, sexy cold dessert like cheesecake or cream pie, something she can slowly drizzle with chocolate syrup right in front of him—no cookies or layer cake."

"You got any?" April asked Monique.

"Any what?"

"Cheesecake, cream pie, cookies, layer cake, chocolate syrup—I'm not particular. I forgot my snack bag at home."

"No, I don't *got* any. Go on, Leigh Ann."

"She should wear something filmy and floral over something substantial like a black tank top and black stretch pants, so it's not obvious that she's thinking about slipping out of it the first chance she gets."

There'd be no "slipping out" of anything except her apartment once Sam had passed out. She didn't need any advice on what to give Sam to knock him out. She'd slipped more mickeys in her books than she could remember, and she knew one that was perfectly safe, that would give him the best night's sleep he'd had in a long time. Jolene had been a bartender in between circus gigs, so she knew how to mix all kinds of concoctions and what their side effects were. True, Jennifer had never tried to put one together in real life, but everything would be fine. Yes, her alibi would be in perfect health and unwilling to admit he'd forgotten the most romantic evening of his entire life. Of course, she'd have to clue him in later, but not while it was happening. She *had* to know if it would work.

"So what do you think?" Leigh Ann asked.

"I think I've got myself a seduction plan," Jennifer said, furiously making notes.

Chapter 16

Jennifer turned her head, and the kiss Sam aimed at her lips fell flat against her cheek. "Not in front of the whole building, sweetheart," she said coyly, nodding her chin toward the Channel 14 receptionist who rolled her eyes skyward.

Jennifer wanted to knee him where it hurt. She wouldn't have Sam playing with her affections—not in public *and* not in private—at least not until she had a mickey to slip him. She didn't need him charging up her hormones. She had Moore to contend with, and she had to stay focused.

"I'll pick you up for lunch at twelve," Sam assured her.

As she turned to head toward the elevator, she felt an unexpected pat on her derriere. She stopped short. She didn't dare turn around. Too many witnesses. Assuming she didn't stab him to death with her fork, lunch would be interesting.

Channel 14's elevator was as ordinary as its lobby, and so were the people in it. So much for the glamour of the biz. She barely recognized Tamara Goodwin, an exotic-looking African-American woman who co-anchored the twelve o'clock news with Steve Moore. She wore no makeup, and without it her almond eyes lost that Egyptian look that made her so striking on the tube. She was dressed in a black turtleneck and jeans. She was both shorter and thinner than Jennifer had thought.

She would have to get used to the idea that Channel 14's beautiful people were not so beautiful at nine A.M.

Down the hall, she passed the weather guy and the sports reporter, both of whose names she'd forgotten, as she made her way to Moore's office, Room 406. The roof, scene of Kyle Browning's suicide/murder, was only a staircase away.

Inside Room 406 a pleasant-looking, middle-aged woman with graying brown hair and large glasses on a chain stopped her with a "May I help you?"

Oh, no. This had to be Edith, the Edith she had threatened over the phone. And she was guarding the way to the two offices in the suite. If God didn't get her for that phone conversation, Edith surely would.

"I'm here to see Mr. Moore," Jennifer said contritely.

"Are you Miss Marsh?" Steely eyes skewered Jennifer.

"Probably, that is, yes."

"Have a seat over there while I tell him you're here."

Jennifer sat down in the rigid molded chair Edith pointed at. Other people got away with being rude and nasty. It wasn't fair.

Jennifer watched as the woman pressed a button on an intercom and announced her arrival. In less than a minute Moore was leading her by the hand into his office. Mentally, she listed the options for disinfecting human flesh. Iodine would leave a stain, but a good swabbing with alcohol might do it.

"I have a feeling this is going to work out well for all of us," Moore insisted, shutting the door behind them.

Jennifer backed up and opened the door a crack. "Sorry.

I'm claustrophobic," she explained. "I can't stand being in closed-in places." *With sex-crazed maniacs like you.*

"Whatever makes you comfortable," he said, his eyes sweeping over her from head to toe, lingering a few seconds here and there. Jennifer fought back an *un*comfortable surge of adrenaline.

"I won't be able to come in tomorrow. I . . . I have an appointment I can't break," Jennifer blurted out. After all, this business of planning a murder, however fake, was demanding, and she had a security system at an apartment building she had to examine.

Moore paused and then smiled. "That's quite all right. I'm sure you're worth waiting for."

Was there nothing she could say to the man without . . .

"You'll be helping me and John with public relations," Moore went on. "Answering letters, fan mail. Securing plane tickets, hotel reservations."

"John?" she asked in a voice a few notes higher than she would have liked.

"John Allen. He's in the adjoining office. He replaced Kyle Browning."

At least the scenery would be pleasant—and she'd have access to Browning's office, not that it was likely to be of much help. All of his belongings would be long gone by now.

"John doesn't come in until eleven most days, since he doesn't go on air until six," Moore explained. "You'll be working in the outer office with Edith. She can show you most of what you need to know. And, of course, I'll have a few special assignments for you."

Mace . . . Mace would be good. She'd have to remember to pick some up this evening.

"I went down to Personnel and got the forms for you."

He handed her a stack of papers half an inch thick. "These are only a formality. You do have a college degree?"

Jennifer nodded, but she wondered why he asked. She had a feeling that the special assignments he had in mind didn't require a degree of any kind, except, perhaps, bad taste.

"Good. Why don't you go ahead and get started on those, so we can get you on the payroll." He ushered her back into the outer office, squeezed her shoulder, and pointed to a desk not five feet from Edith's. "That's your work station. Let me know if you need anything."

Moore threw her one last leer, returned to his office, and shut the door.

A stun gun. She could definitely use a stun gun.

Jennifer sighed and sat down at the desk. She also needed the answer to who killed Kyle Browning, and she'd like to get it before Moore got what *he* wanted. She began leafing through the stack of papers.

"When's the audit?" Edith asked.

"I beg your pardon?" Jennifer said innocently, hoping Edith had mistaken her for someone from accounting.

"The job audit."

Couldn't the woman cut her some slack? "Sorry about that. But I need this job, and I—"

Edith chuckled. "Think so, huh? We'll see how bad you need it. Moore runs through temps like soap stars run through tissues. If they stay a week, we think we're doing well. But if you want to work for Moore, that's your business."

"*You* work for him."

"I work for the station."

"And you worked for Kyle Browning?" Jennifer asked.

Edith eyed her suspiciously. "We've been told not to talk about the incident with Mr. Browning."

"I wasn't asking about the *incident*. I was asking about the man. He was my favorite Channel 14 news anchor," she said earnestly. "When I turn on the tube at six o'clock, I miss hearing him."

And in all truth, she did. Browning exuded a rare kind of Walter Cronkite sincerity and confidence. She didn't miss seeing him, however. She could watch John Allen give the news with her TV on mute. In fact, he was better on mute.

Edith sighed, and her veneer of distrust seemed to weaken. "Yes, I worked for him. We started out together."

"In New York?"

"Yes."

"How'd he wind up in Macon?"

Edith's face softened. "Kyle was originally from Macon. He and Steve had been friends for many years, but I bet you didn't know that."

She didn't know that. She didn't even know Browning was from Georgia. If he'd ever shared any of the local accent, he lost it well before he was broadcasting in New York.

"But why'd he come back?"

"He never told me."

"But you came with him. You must have some idea."

Darn! She'd gone one step too far, too soon. She could see the openness in Edith's eyes cloud again with wariness. This would never have happened to Maxie Malone. If she could only page up in her word processor and rewrite this scene, maybe she could get it right.

"You'd better get those forms filled out and down to Human Resources this morning."

Jennifer sighed. She'd not be getting much more out of Edith. At least, not for a while.

She shuffled through the papers. IRS withholding, one exemption. Too bad she couldn't count Muffy. She ate like an exemption. Social Security number, address, phone.

" 'Home is the place where, when you have to go there, they have to take you in,' " Edith stated.

"I beg your pardon," Jennifer said.

"It's a quote from Robert Frost's 'The Death of the Hired Man.' You asked why Kyle Browning came back to Macon."

Chapter 17

Some lunch! Sam owed her more than a salad from Kroger's even if he *had* carefully selected each item, made sure he included spinach (to which he had an admitted personal aversion), topped it with shredded cheese and croutons, and smothered it in her favorite blue cheese dressing.

Jennifer stuffed another spoonful into her mouth and crunched into bean sprouts. Yum. And just because it was delicious—her tongue found a black olive to join the party of flavors—was no reason for Sam to think she actually liked eating outside in a park on a gorgeous spring day. She'd had something in mind like a thirty dollar entrée at one of Macon's exclusive restaurants. He owed her big-time for putting up with Moore, and she intended to see him pay.

Sam bit off a third of his hamburger, wiped his mouth with a napkin, and took a big slurp of the supersize cola that sat perched on the wooden park bench. "What's it like on the battlefront?"

Jennifer swallowed and took a drink of the flavored water Sam had brought her. Blackberry—the best. "I don't know how much I can find out. Moore seems to have only one thing on his mind when I'm in the room."

"I can understand that." Sam gave her an approving scan. "But then that means he's not suspicious of you. After all, he came to you, not you to him."

And you to me, she thought.

Jennifer made the mistake of looking him straight in those gorgeous eyes of his. She was angry with him, but she couldn't remember why.

"I want you to see if you can gain access to the files."

"I've got access. As a matter of fact, filing is one of the menial jobs they threw my way. They didn't even ask me if I knew the alphabet."

"Good. Go through them as carefully as you can."

"And find what? What am I looking for?" Jennifer asked petulantly. "And Edith seems cemented in her chair."

"She has to go to the bathroom sometime. Do it then. Look for notes on an investigative report that was never aired, one that happened during the time that Browning was at the station."

"I haven't exactly memorized Channel 14's news broadcasts, you know. But if you think we're looking for something to do with a news report, I think you're wrong. Moore's a reader, not a reporter. He messed around all morning, and then at eleven-thirty a young Jimmy Olson type came into the office carrying a script. Moore took it into the office. I could hear him reading through it."

"So you think Browning was a reader, too?"

Jennifer shrugged. "Who knows? But they replaced him with John Allen—that should be a big hint."

"Well, check the files anyway. You never know. Browning started out as a field reporter, but that was more than a few years ago. Also keep an ear out for who Browning socialized with."

"Do you have any idea how hard it is to start a conversation about a dead man's social life?"

"You've only been there a few hours. I have complete confidence in you."

"Do you, now?"

"Yeah, I do."

She shook her head. She didn't like the way her mind wandered when she was around Sam. She kept getting distracted by minor things like his teeth. They had character. And his chin, while strong, had just a hint of vulnerability . . .

". . . to get a look at that roof, if possible," Sam was saying.

Why did men insist on talking? Jennifer drew her mind back to Kyle Browning. The man was dead. He deserved at least a bit of her attention.

Her characters never had trouble keeping on track. Maxie Malone was sharp as a tack—always. And Jolene, well, when Jolene met some guy, she just got *it* over with and never let *it* interfere with an investigation.

She stuffed a cracker into her mouth and mumbled, "Should have saved the picnic for tomorrow." Eating usually brought her mind back to reality.

"Why?"

"We could eat on the roof. If anyone catches us, it'll look like a romantic tryst."

Sam gave her a sly smile and slurped cola through his straw. "Sounds good to me. I'll bring the food; you bring yourself."

She hated how he did that, how he left her without a

comeback, how he made her so acutely aware of her femininity.

"I'd better get you back to work. Moore will wonder what's happened to you. I don't want him getting suspicious. We don't know what part Moore may have had in Browning's death."

Jennifer got her big chance to search the files at four o'clock when a breathless, red-faced young woman came begging for help. A major paper jam had developed in the Xerox machine down the hall. Edith scurried off, leaving the files unguarded.

Jennifer had passed Moore in the hall on her way back into the building. He told her he was on his way out to lunch. He hadn't come back. She was alone in the office.

She immediately flew to the cabinet where she pulled each and every file and found . . . nothing. Nothing was in the files. Nothing except things like when and where Moore last spoke to the Woman's Club or Allen helped open a supermarket, and, of course, various flight schedules and trips.

Just as Jennifer was slipping the last folder back into place, John Allen walked through the door. She slammed the drawer shut.

Allen stared at Jennifer, looked back toward the hall, and then back at Jennifer. "Do I know you?" he asked, screwing up his face as though he were looking into the sun. He was dressed in a Bulldogs T-shirt and walking shorts.

"Jennifer Marsh," she said, offering her hand. "I'm your new assistant."

His grip was mushy.

"Yeah, well, the turnover is pretty big around here.

Most of you don't last long enough for me to remember your names. But you look kind of familiar . . ."

"Happens all the time," Jennifer insisted. "It's the face." She pointed at herself. "Very common face." She didn't want to deal with his recognizing her as the caterer at Moore's party, but it didn't look as if she'd have to. No flashes were going off in that dull brain.

"Did they bring my clothes?" he asked, running a hand over his chin and ruffling through his hair.

Jennifer nodded. "A jacket, shirt, and tie. I hung them on the back of your office door."

"Did they bring cuff links? Last time they sent French cuffs without any links. I had to use safety pins. I spent the whole newscast trying to keep the sleeve of the sport jacket from riding up too high."

Poor baby. This news business was tough. "No cuff links and no French cuffs."

"Any mail?"

"It's on your desk. Two fan letters." (She assumed business letters didn't come with red heart stickers and a big red lipstick print over the seal.) "And a credit card bill."

Allen mumbled, went to his office, and shut the door behind him.

Jennifer let out a sigh. She had one more place she wanted to look before Edith got that copier machine back in order.

She slipped behind Edith's desk and pulled out the file drawer on the bottom right. Neatly arranged one after the other were unlabeled manila folders. Jennifer pulled out the first one. Inside were all sizes of scrap paper with handwritten notes, all having to do with Channel 14 and the news department. A few names caught her eye, including Steve Moore and Kyle Browning.

"Don't use that kind of paper. Throw it away if you can't keep it out of the stacks with the regular stock." Edith's voice echoed down the hall.

Jennifer dumped the folder back into the drawer and flew to her own desk as Edith came through the door.

"I don't have time this late in the day to become a maintenance supervisor. Has he come in yet?" She motioned toward Allen's door.

Jennifer nodded.

"The clothes here?"

Again Jennifer nodded.

"I'll give him a few more minutes. He has to be inspected before he goes down to makeup. The man doesn't even know how to knot his own tie."

Edith sat down behind her desk, pulled open the lap drawer, and extracted a pack of cigarettes and some matches. She lit one with shaky hands and turned a steely stare at Jennifer. "I'm smoking this here and now, and I don't give a hoot what you or any regulations say." She took a deep breath, burning down a good half inch of the cigarette, and flicked the ashes in an ashtray inside the drawer.

Jennifer hated cigarette smoke—she got enough of it at the private parties she and Dee Dee catered—but Edith obviously needed something to calm her nerves. She looked to be in a dangerous state.

After two more puffs Edith's hands stopped shaking and some of the misery seemed to drain from her face. She stamped out the butt and shut the drawer.

"Sometimes I feel like I'm working in a nursery school. I have two big kids I've got to get dressed and made presentable five days a week." She laughed bitterly. "Some job, huh?"

A thought crept into Jennifer's mind. Did she dare say it? "Did you ever want to be part of the talent?"

Edith hesitated a moment, considering. "I started out as a journalist. I worked for a newspaper for five years. It folded, and then I thought, why not try TV? I should have looked in the mirror first."

It wasn't that Edith was unattractive. She had good features and nice hair if only she'd do something with it. And she'd have to lose those horrible, thick-framed glasses. She might actually be quite pretty—in person. But she'd never have that star quality, that charisma that had to make itself felt across the long cable from studio to TV set.

"If that's why you're here . . ." Edith gave her a long, appraising look, "Oh, hell, go for it. I'd be the last one to discourage anyone from going after their dreams."

"Do you still write?"

Jennifer had hit a nerve. She knew it as soon as she said it. That cloudy anger rose back up, close to the surface of Edith's features.

"Why would I write? Just what do you think someone like me would have to write about?"

Chapter 18

Jennifer shoved the reading glasses back up on the bridge of her nose, patted the black curls of her wig into place, and pressed the doorbell to Mrs. Walker's apartment. The first stanza of "Georgia" echoed through the door. A few seconds later she heard the dead bolt slide back and another lock turn. Immediately, a snarling ball of miniature mutt attacked her shoes.

"Isn't that sweet? Tiger is so glad to see you. Won't you come in, Sophie? Let me take that sweater for you."

"No, I'm fine. I tend to be chilly." Jennifer clutched the misshapen cardigan around her, fearful that without it she'd look like a shoplifter from Macy's linen department.

"I see you're well bolted in," Jennifer said, examining the locks on the door. "Are these all standard or did you have some added? I'd like to think you were safe with all the crime we hear about these days."

"The locks came with the door. We're not allowed to put anything on ourselves. But you don't have to worry, dear. This is a secure building. Ernie won't let anyone in he doesn't know. I told him you were coming this morning. You didn't have any problems, did you?" Mrs. Walker continued to wipe her hands on the towel she held. Her red gingham apron showed signs of what looked like ketchup across the bib.

Jennifer shook her head. The doorman had greeted her by name when she arrived a few minutes ago, and she felt certain he would let her in anytime, whether Mrs. Walker told him she was coming or not.

Ernie was particularly concerned about Jennifer's condition. His niece had given birth to her firstborn while stuck in city traffic in a taxicab. Since then, he assured her, he had taken a first-aid class that included "birthing babies." He seemed anxious to put that training to the test. Not a reassuring thought.

He had put Jennifer in the elevator and even offered to go up with her. He couldn't have been nicer without handing her the key to apartment 1129.

Jennifer ran her hand over Mrs. Walker's door frame. One dead bolt, one standard lock. She could easily get past the standard lock. Her serial killer, the vile, demented Marcus, knew how to slip one in less than five seconds. That's why she had him kill people who lived in older houses. This new type of dead bolt would be a problem. It was state of the art with a good, two-inch bolt. Unfortunately, the only breaking and entering experience she had outside of her own apartment was on paper, and a real lock wouldn't open by typing "the lock gave way" or "the bolt slid cleanly back into its housing." She'd been fudging too long with her writing. She had to find some real way to defeat a lock like this one.

"Come along, dear. You need to get that weight off your feet. We don't want your ankles swelling up like balloons."

Jennifer followed Mrs. Walker into the living room, Tiger nipping at her heels.

"I made lasagna. I thought your grandmother probably made it for you, and I want you to feel right at home here."

The only lasagna served at Jennifer's grandmother's house had come out of the frozen food section of the grocery store. Grandma had made fried chicken, mashed potatoes, gravy, and homemade biscuits. Jennifer had savored those Sunday dinners. Of course, that was before Grandma discovered the wonders of refrigerated biscuits and canned gravy. And before Jennifer had had her philosophical awakening about meat.

"It smells delicious," Jennifer assured her, sitting down, the distinct odor of Italian sausage filling the apartment. If the sausage chunks were big enough, she could pick them out. Otherwise, she'd try to isolate the noodle/cheese layers from the sauce. If all else failed, she could always plead morning sickness.

"Can I give you a hand?" Jennifer offered.

"Oh, no. It'll be in the oven for another ten minutes. The salad is in the fridge, and I just popped in the garlic bread."

Mrs. Walker sat down close to Jennifer on the sofa, seemingly oblivious to the diminutive monster who had caught his spindly incisor in the woven leather of Jennifer's shoe right next to her little toe. Jennifer had to get the woman out of the room.

"Could I have a glass of water?" Jennifer croaked.

Mrs. Walker patted her knee. "You most certainly may. I've got some nice bottled springwater in the pantry. I'll be back in a shake."

As soon as Mrs. Walker cleared the doorway, Jennifer took hold of Tiger, disengaged his tooth from her shoe, and held him high in the air. "I thought we had an understanding." He growled his disagreement.

She had to keep him off of her, but she didn't know any way short of sacrificing one of her shoes. Limping back to Macon was not part of her game plan. She looked pitiful enough already.

With her free hand she frantically searched through her purse. Her hand closed on a leather glove, and she pulled it out.

She lifted the skirt on the sofa and tossed the glove under it, shoving Tiger in after, just as Mrs. Walker returned with a large tea glass of sparkling water.

"There you are, dear." She looked about the floor. "Has Tiger disappeared again? It's strange, but many times when I have company, I'll step out of the room for just a moment, and the little darling vanishes."

Jennifer just bet he did.

The sofa emitted a muffled rumble.

"Did you hear something?" Mrs. Walker asked.

"It's just my stomach. I had a light breakfast, and the smell of your cooking is making me hungry."

"Good for you, dear. You must nourish our little one and drink plenty of water. It's absolutely essential."

Jennifer took a sip from the glass and placed it on the coffee table. She now had an idea of Penney Richmond's front door security. The only other way into the apartment was a small balcony. Maybe it would offer easier access.

Jennifer put a hand to her mouth, closed her eyes, tried to think *pale*, and fanned her free hand rapidly in front of her face. "I think I need some air. Do you mind if I . . ." She motioned toward the spectacular view.

"No, of course not. Feeling a little queasy, are we?"

Jennifer gulped back a reply having to do with just who *we* were and followed the older woman to the windows. The glass gave the impression of standing on a precipice, a clear drop of twelve stories to the ground.

The door to the balcony was custom-built and looked like one more large, double-paned panel. The lock was standard. Security had been pretty lax when they put in these doors, or so Jennifer thought, until she stepped outside into the cacophony of downtown Atlanta.

"I don't come out here too often," Mrs. Walker yelled.

"I can understand why." Jennifer could also see why security had scrimped on the balcony lock. The narrow platform was not much more than a two-person perch above the city. It was about six feet long and wrapped to the left around the brick wall so as not to obstruct the view of the windows.

Each balcony was a considerable distance from the other, spanning most of the length of the apartment, way too far to leap from one to another. But the balconies beneath all lay in a straight, vertical line. Someone with mountain-climbing equipment could make their way up fairly easily. Don a black turtleneck, sweatpants, a cap, a little soot on the face—piece of cake—for Sylvester Stallone. In her current physical condition—exercise was something to be watched and appreciated aesthetically—Jennifer couldn't get past the patio on the first floor. And heights—well, she thought she was just fine with heights until she took a peek over the railing.

"Just look at you! You're turning green!" Mrs. Walker shouted above the din. "This air isn't good for you." She pulled Jennifer back inside and shut the door, cutting off the noise. "Sometimes I think you have no concern about your condition," she scolded.

Jennifer was very concerned about her condition and the prospect of losing her breakfast on Mrs. Walker's white carpet. She lowered herself carefully onto the couch, all the time swallowing air in little gulps. At last her stomach muscles began to relax.

"That's better. We've got some color back in our cheeks," Mrs. Walker assured her.

The timer dinged in the kitchen just as the doorbell sang out "Georgia."

"Would you mind getting that?" Mrs. Walker asked. "If I don't get the casserole out right away, the noodles at the edges turn into something resembling cement." Not an appetizing analogy.

Jennifer went to the door and peered through the peep-hole. A young woman stood there shifting back and forth, her eyes darting up and down the hall and back to a piece of paper she clutched in her fist. Jennifer opened the door.

"I'm really sorry to bother you, but I was looking for 1235 and I can't seem—"

"Go back to the elevator and go all the way down to the lobby," Mrs. Walker called from the end of the hall. "Then take an elevator on the opposite side of the hall."

"You mean I can't get there from here?"

Mrs. Walker came up beside Jennifer. "No. The building is separated into two distinct wings. You've got to go all the way down."

"Thank you. I'm so sorry to have bothered you."

"No problem," Mrs. Walker assured her, shutting and locking the door. She sighed.

"Does that happen often?" Jennifer asked. "People getting lost like that?"

"Once a month or so, I guess. Ernie gives them directions, but it's confusing. We've all gotten used to it. I just redirect them. We all do."

"We?"

"The residents. If I'm alone, I look to make sure it's some nonthreatening-looking person before I open the door."

What could be less threatening than a young, pregnant woman who bore a haunting resemblance to a near-sighted Snow White?

Maybe she wouldn't have to break in. All she had to do was to get Penney Richmond to open the door. That should be easy enough if Ms. Richmond had half the confidence in the downstairs security that Mrs. Walker had. And if she was used to directing traffic back and forth between the two halves of the building. And if the directions ruse didn't work, she could always pretend to go into labor. Surely, even a hard-hearted creature like Penney Richmond would open her door to a young woman giving birth. And that was all she had to do—get Penney to open the door, like in a game of tag.

Chapter 19

Alone at last! And it was only ten o'clock. Moore and Edith had been called to a meeting, and Jennifer was left to cover the phones. John Allen had yet to show up. He apparently wasn't required to attend the regular Thursday morning staff meetings, and, if Tuesday were any indication, he wouldn't be in until well after lunch. She had Allen's office all to herself.

She went straight to the wooden desk in the center of the room and flipped through the appointment calendar that lay on top. *Lunch* and *Drinks* seemed to be his main activities, along with several appointments with a well-known orthodontist.

The lap drawer contained some loose change, paper clips, half a dozen pens, and a ruler. The side drawers were filled with Channel 14 stationery and blank tablets. They looked as if they hadn't been disturbed since they were put there. Allen was either the neatest person she had ever encountered, which she doubted, or he didn't do much work in the office.

Jennifer abandoned the desk for the bookcases that lined the back wall. They were filled with history books, atlases, and political works, along with personal biographies of newsmen like David Brinkley and Walter Cronkite. Even Howard Cosell's book was there. She drew one out and opened the cover. The book was signed by the author with *To Kyle* scrawled across the top. Hah! So whoever cleaned out Browning's belongings skipped the bookcase.

She jerked open the doors to the covered area below. The shelves were bare except for three laser-paper boxes. The first was stationery personalized with Browning's name and the station's address. The second held plain sheets. The third was almost empty, but the top sheet was filled with print. She dumped out the small stack and took it back to Allen's desk.

My Life as a News Anchor by Kyle Browning was centered on two lines above the first page of type. It began: "Growing up poor in Macon, Georgia, I never thought I would amount to anything."

Jennifer scanned the first five pages, at the end of which little Kyle was walking and all of eighteen months old. The manuscript was forty-four pages long.

Jennifer flipped to the last page. "I didn't go to my senior prom. Natalie Morgan turned me down."

So old Kyle was a late bloomer; so late in some areas, his literary skills had yet to sprout. Browning was famous for reducing a major news story to a three-minute report. Too bad he couldn't recognize the high points in his own life.

She started to slip the manuscript back into the box when she noticed a brown, nine-by-twelve-inch envelope folded in the bottom. It was addressed by hand to *Kyle Browning* with no return address. So even celebrities had to send self-addressed, stamped envelopes when submitting to a publisher or an agent.

The envelope bore an Atlanta postmark. Jennifer

unfolded it and slipped out an 8½ x11 sheet of paper. She recognized it immediately. It was one of those infuriating standard rejections:

Dear Writer

Thank you for thinking of the Penney Richmond Literary Agency. We've read your work with interest, but I'm sorry to say it's not right for us at this time. We wish you luck in placing your manuscript with an agency that can give your work the enthusiasm it deserves.

Across the bottom, in pen, was scrawled:

Kyle, you've got to be kidding, sweetheart. It was a joke, wasn't it? Burn this thing and start over—and remember, what people want to read is the dirt, sweetie. You've got a name big enough to carry a bestseller, but you've got to tell your readers the story they want to hear, not whether or not you ate your peas and carrots as a kid. Do it, Kyle. Just do it. P.R.

So Penney Richmond was an equal opportunity S.O.B., insulting the famous along with the unknown.

Jennifer closed the box and took it back to her desk, where she slipped the manuscript and the letter into the tote bag in her drawer.

She wasn't really stealing, she rationalized. After all, Browning was dead, and dead people can't own property, at least under the law. And if anyone else had wanted it, surely they would have taken it by now. Aw, heck! What was one more cracked Commandment?

She heard Moore and Edith chatting as they came down the hall. She grabbed the first object her fingers touched, a desk calendar, and started frantically flipping through it.

Moore stopped at her desk and leaned down. "Busy?" he asked, the faintest whiff of alcohol escaping with his breath.

"I was just checking the holidays," she babbled. "Easter comes on a Sunday this year."

"You don't say." Moore chuckled. "Come into the office. I've got a little project I want you to help me with."

All right, so where was Sam, her protector, the guy who assured her Moore could be handled? She opened her lap drawer to take out a notebook.

"Don't bother. You won't be needing that."

No, she'd probably need a billy club or a baseball bat. Unfortunately, neither was handy.

Edith threw her a knowing look but offered no help. Moore was standing at his door, holding it open. She had no choice but to go inside. Moore followed her and let the door fall shut.

She felt his hands on her waist and his chin scrape against her cheek as he nuzzled her neck. She ducked away and put the full length of the desk between them, hoping Moore wouldn't stoop to actually chasing her around it. How clichéd could he get?

But he just looked at her with his dazzling smile and pointed to a chair. "Have a seat," he suggested as though he hadn't just committed a sexual offense of one degree or another.

"My book will be out next month, and I have a seven-city book-signing tour in the works: New York, Chicago, Washington, etcetera. I'll be needing an assistant, a traveling companion to keep things in order. I thought you might like to—"

No, she would *not* like to do whatever his lust-crazed mind might invent. And she had no intentions of flying all over the country with a man old enough to be her father who had anything but fatherly feelings toward her. She needed an out, and she needed it now.

"Muffy," Jennifer blurted out. "I can't leave Muffy alone."

"And who is Muffy? Your roommate?"

Jennifer nodded. "She lives with me."

"What's wrong with her? Can't she feed herself?"

"No, she can't. She can't go out of the apartment without me. I even have to bathe her."

"What's wrong with the poor creature?"

Jennifer paused for a moment. "I guess you might say it's a genetic condition."

"Doesn't she have any family?"

"Not that I know of."

"And you've taken on her entire care yourself?"

Again Jennifer nodded. "She's like family to me. She was going to die, and I took her in." Real tears gathered in the corners of her eyes.

Moore cleared his throat. He actually seemed moved. Maybe he wasn't a complete sleazeball after all. "I understand. I know what it's like to face the loss of a dear friend."

"I suppose you and Kyle Browning were close."

"I knew Kyle for most of my life. He and I went to high school together. We both wanted to be newsmen, but who would have thought that one of us would actually reach the top."

"I'm sure Mr. Browning had quite a story to tell." Here it was, her opening to find out what Moore knew about

Kyle's ill-fated manuscript. "Too bad he never published a book about his life."

"You want to know about Kyle Browning?"

Jennifer nodded vigorously.

"I suppose you're curious why a man like that would jump off a building. You, no doubt, followed the accounts of what happened in North Carolina."

Again she nodded.

"Tell you what. I'll give you an autographed copy of my book as soon as it comes out. The real story—it's all in there. You just wait and see."

Chapter 20

It wasn't Luigi's, but it would do. A crisp wind whipped across the top of the Channel 14 building, lifting the corners of the red-checked, cotton tablecloth that Sam had spread almost in the middle of the flat roof. He anchored one edge with his briefcase, a second with the rattan picnic basket, and the other two with a bottle of wine and a loaf of Italian bread. Then he motioned for Jennifer to have a seat.

"Don't you want to look around first?" Jennifer asked, settling down on her knees and sifting through the contents of the basket. Oooooh. A seasoned salad and what looked like vegetable lasagna were teasing her nose with garlic and oregano. Underneath was a covered dish containing something that looked suspiciously like chocolate mousse. So it wasn't Italian. Mousse spoke a universal language.

"Let's set the scene first," Sam suggested, "just in case someone decides to come up here. It's too beautiful a day to take chances."

Jennifer could live with that. She intended to eat the goodies in that basket before her lunch hour was up, and she certainly had no problem making it sooner than later.

"I would have brought candles, but I didn't think we

could get away with lighting them with the breeze," Sam said.

It didn't matter that it was high noon. Candles were a pleasant thought. But Sam was right. They would no more get them lit when the wind would topple them and send their lunch up in smoke.

"Would you like to serve or shall I?" he asked.

"You pour the wine. I'll take care of the food," Jennifer offered, pulling out the container of salad and dividing it equally into two plastic bowls. She dug in the bottom of the basket and came up with two full services of real silverware. She traded Sam his bowl and a salad fork for a glass of wine and then took up her own serving, munching noisily on the crisp greens.

"Did you get anything out of Moore?" Sam asked.

"He told me to read his book. He's going to give me my very own autographed copy."

"How thoughtful."

Jennifer sighed. "So what do you think we'll find up here?" She stuffed a second forkful into her mouth. The dressing wasn't quite as good as her own, but it was passable.

"Probably nothing, but I thought it might be helpful to get the lay of the land, determine how difficult it would be to fall off this building."

"Or be pushed," Jennifer added.

"Or be pushed," Sam agreed.

"Do you have time for lunch like this every day?" she asked, tearing off half the loaf of bread and tossing a chunk to Sam.

He caught it and shook his head. "I don't eat lunch. Too much to do. Right now I'm running down last night's arrests. Can't you tell?"

"Can you get away with taking time off like this?" She gestured at their salads.

Sam shrugged. "I'll make it up tonight. I don't have to have my copy in until late, and the police department never closes. It's just that I like to have my articles in early enough to pretend I have a normal job, so I can at least catch a decent supper now and then."

"You love it, don't you?" Jennifer observed, catching a glimpse of passion in Sam's eyes.

"It has its rewards, but what I do is still only a job. What you do is more of a calling."

A calling that she sometimes wished would go call someone else.

"When did you start writing stories?" Sam asked.

Jennifer took his empty bowl and stuffed it along with her own into a plastic bag. Then she pulled out the lasagna and cut it in two, slipping each half onto a plastic plate. He took his and dove into the cheesy layers.

"I honestly don't remember. I didn't start with the mysteries until I was out of college. I tried working in advertising for two years and then my parents died. I sold their house, put the money in a small trust fund, and moved into the apartment where I live now. The fund almost pays the rent. Dee Dee was looking for someone to help her when she started the catering business, and it seemed a perfect fit. If I wanted to write for a living, I had to commit most of my time to it. Of course that was almost five years and eight novels ago."

"Are you any good?"

Now just how was she supposed to answer a question like that? "Of course I'm good. At least, good enough. Why do you ask?"

"Five years is a long time. You must have had doubts.

But if you can still say you're good, you have something far more important than talent."

Gall?

"Persistence," Sam continued. "You don't make it in a business like publishing without determination."

He was right there. Determination and many reams of paper.

"And you? Did you ever want to write fiction?"

"Naw. I'm doing what I want, searching out the truth, telling it like it is with as little bias as I can manage. Sounds corny, doesn't it?"

Actually it sounded wonderful. Most of the people she'd met in the newspaper business had become jaded. Sam, somehow, had remained a believer.

He smiled, a shy, confessional smile, and her heart jumped a little.

She *had* to keep her mission in mind. Her relationship with Sam *had* to be strictly business. She couldn't afford to get sidetracked. She needed a man to seduce. Unfortunately, it had to be Sam, this true believer. There was nobody else.

"Do you think you could come by my apartment Friday night, say about seven o'clock? I want to talk to you about laying out the book about Browning, decide how we're going to divide up the labor."

Sam nodded. "Sounds fine."

"I'll fix something to eat. I know you won't have time to grab anything before that."

"That seals it. I can be bought."

She hoped so.

Jennifer glanced at her watch. "It's getting late. I have to be back downstairs in half an hour."

Sam wiped his mouth with a paper napkin and helped

her dispose of the rest of their dishes. "The last thing we want is someone to come looking for you." He stood up, offered her his hand, and pulled her to her feet.

"The mousse," she said plaintively.

"You can take it with you for an afternoon break. Tell you what: I'll even throw in my serving. But you've got to earn it."

They scoured the side of the building that overlooked the parking lot but found nothing. No bloodstains, murder weapons, or other telltale signs of mayhem. Not that Jennifer actually expected anything of substance, but she had hoped for a button ripped from the murderer's jacket. Almost every TV detective who lasted more than one season had at least one case that hinged on a button. Real life was so much harder than fiction.

Sam began to inspect the wall itself. It ran around the entire roof and was close to three feet high. Jennifer peeked over the edge. It was a long way down.

"Look at how narrow this is," she said. "If you climbed up on this wall, it wouldn't be thick enough for you to stand on. It certainly wouldn't be wide enough for a man who was over six feet tall."

"So, what's your point?"

"Don't you think someone who is about to commit suicide wants to stand there for a moment, on the precipice, contemplating what he's about to do, before taking the plunge?"

"What is this? You think the guy's going to go around town looking for a place to perch before he takes the dive? Come on. Besides, he could have swung his legs over and sat on the top."

"Are you kidding? He'd fall off."

"Which he did. The question is whether or not he had help."

"Stand here," Jennifer ordered, positioning Sam with the back of his legs against the wall. "Look where your center of gravity, your abdomen, falls. It's above the rim."

"So one strong push . . ."

"And over you'd tumble."

"Straight into the parking lot below."

She leaned over for another look with Sam standing so close to her she could almost feel his heart beating beneath his jacket.

And then she was in his arms, and he was kissing her passionately like one of those crazy, irrational moments in one of Leigh Ann's novels that never, ever happen in real life. One of those moments when a man does exactly what a woman wants him to do, exactly what she dreamed he would do but never does. . . .

"I hate to break up the party," a deep voice bellowed.

Jennifer wasn't talking and neither was Sam. His mouth was too busy. Where were those words coming from?

"No one's allowed up here."

Sam loosened his grip and whispered into Jennifer's ear, "Sorry about that. He was coming up on us fast and I didn't have time to explain."

Explain? What did he need to explain?

She turned to face a white-haired man dressed in the uniform of a security guard.

"I hate to . . . uh . . . disturb you two. Looks like you were having quite a lunch up here. But since Browning took a leap off this roof, the brass doesn't want anybody up here. Too big a liability risk."

"Sorry, officer," Sam said. "We didn't know. We'll clear up our mess and get out of your way."

The man followed them back to the tablecloth, where Sam and Jennifer bent down and began gathering up their belongings.

"Were you on duty the day that Browning went over?" Sam asked.

"Yeah." The man shuddered. "It was quite a mess. His head cracked open like a cantaloupe."

Wonderful image, especially for a caterer.

"I don't guess any of you were really shocked, though," Jennifer suggested, corking the wine and lowering it into the basket. "I mean, he must have been depressed for some time to take his life like that."

"Depressed? Not that I know of. I talked to him just that morning. He seemed like he always did, only he had an interview with some celebrity for the evening news. I forget now who it was. But he was looking forward to it, some old friend of his and a real coup for the station. Yes sir, if he was going to kill himself, I think he would have picked another day."

Chapter 21

The room breathed seduction. Maybe gasped was more like it. Jennifer had been aiming for something like a scene in one of Leigh Ann's better novels, but she had a more contemporary setting in mind, not a medieval romance.

The room was dark, lit only by pink forty-watt bulbs that were supposed to bathe the apartment in a soft, otherworldly glow but created something more like a dim "Oh, God, I'm going blind" effect.

A cluster of candles on the coffee table formed a bright pocket of light around a fishbowl of stemless, floating carnations. The critique group would give her a D− for the carnations, but the supermarket was all out of everything else, except for daisies. She'd gone with the carnations.

Maybe Sam wouldn't notice. If she played her part right, Sam wouldn't remember anything about the night except that she had been there.

Mentally, Jennifer went down her checklist. The wine was chilling in the refrigerator, and Celtic harp music was barely audible in the background. The salads were on ice, a loaf of Dee Dee's best bread was sliced and waiting along with the ingredients for a quick pasta dish—assuming they made it to the entrée. The sleeping pills were ground into a fine powder and sat waiting on the kitchen counter, enough to make Sam really, really relaxed when mixed with a little wine. She'd have to make sure he didn't take too much alcohol.

She'd planned it all so perfectly. Everything should go fine. Everything *would* go fine as long as Sam didn't kiss her like he had on the roof.

The doorbell rang. Jennifer grabbed up a sheer black shirt and slipped it over her black tank top and stretch pants. She straightened her collar, tossed back her long, wavy hair—men, she'd been told, loved women's hair long and down—and touched the corner of her eye where the liner and the shadow made a dramatic upward curve. Eye makeup made her eyes swell if she wore it too often, but she felt it was necessary tonight.

She drew in a deep breath and threw back the door lock. *Ready or not, Sam Culpepper, you are about to be seduced.*

Sam greeted her with a puzzled, open-mouthed stare. "Jennifer?"

The cad. He could at least have thrown her a leer.

"Sam," she beamed, her mouth twitching at the corners as she consciously tried to take the plastic out of her smile. She took his hand, pulled him inside, and shut and locked the door behind him. The fly was in the parlor.

She watched as his eyes traveled from the coffee table to the stereo to the dining table set with china—she owned only two good plates and two crystal water goblets, a gift from her mother to seed her hope chest. He arched an eyebrow. "I thought we were going to talk about the book."

She dropped his hand. She might as well have pinned a sign across her chest reading TAKE ME, YOU FOOL!

Her instincts told her to rip open the door, shove him

back into the hall, and lock it after him. But she couldn't. She had to experience that gritty, real-life adrenaline rush of the criminal. And she needed Sam—not *needed* him, just plain, ordinary needed him—here, in her bed, all night.

She reached for his jacket. He shrugged it off and handed it to her. She hung it on the doorknob of the closet. "I thought you might like a little something before we talk," she purred, taking his arm and pulling him into the living area. She'd listened to enough of Leigh Ann's dialogue. If she could just get the words out without gagging, she should have enough lines stored up to at least get her through an hour with Sam, or however long it took him to pass out.

"A little something?" Sam repeated.

Damn! English majors and journalists were *so* literal.

She leaned against him and whispered up toward his ear, "Wine."

There was that stirring inside her again. How was she going to get close to this man and keep her objectivity if he sent butterflies racing to her nether reaches every time she was within six inches of him?

"Wine would be good."

Jennifer pushed Sam down onto the couch and reached for his collar. He folded his hand around hers.

"I'm just loosening your tie," she explained. He relaxed his grip but left his hand lightly folded over hers as she slid down the knot and unclasped his top button. She felt his grip tighten, and a tiny ball of panic formed in her stomach.

"I'll get that wine and be back in just a minute," she promised.

Jennifer escaped to the kitchen, where she shuddered

against the counter. Was she out of her mind? She should have Steve Moore out there on her couch. She could run faster than he could, and she didn't have any problems staying on task around him—or stuffing him with sleeping pills. She had a funnel in the kitchen cabinet.

She shook the ground-up powder into a blue, long-stemmed glass, paused and then scooped out a little with a spoon. She didn't want to give him too much. She filled the glass with wine and then poured the pink one for herself. She'd seen too many whodunits—not to mention Danny Kaye's flagon-with-the-dragon, chalice-with-the-palace, vessel-with-the-pestle routine—where the drugged glass got switched to leave herself guessing which one had the pills. Blue was for boys; pink was for girls.

She swirled the red wine with a spoon until all of the white bits had disappeared, and then carried the glasses back to the couch. Sam was sitting stretched back with his eyes closed.

"You asleep?" she asked.

His eyes slowly opened. "I was just wondering how the accident happened."

"The accident?"

"The one where I died and went to Heaven."

It was corny; it was stupid. If anyone else had said it, it would have made her mad.

She handed him the blue wineglass. He took a small sip and set it down on the coffee table. His arm was stretched out across the back of the couch, waiting. Jennifer took a big swig of wine and sat down next to him, her knee touching his. She stared at the wineglass she held in her lap. She felt his gaze travel over her profile and down the soft curls of her hair.

"I admire you," he said softly.

She whipped her head around to look at him in the gray light, that hair of his falling loose over one eyebrow, his dark eyes shining black in the dim light, and a sweet half smile on his face. He reached for his wine and took another sip.

"You what?" she asked.

He shook his head. "You heard me."

"Why?"

"Because you have the courage to do what you want to do and because you won't let anyone tell you that you can't."

"Maybe I'm just stupid," she suggested.

He shook his head. "You're smart, you're damn good, and you know it. And it'll happen for you one day."

"Why do you say that?"

"Because it has to. Because you won't give up."

Because you're willing to do anything—including pulling a ridiculous stunt like this—to make it happen.

Jennifer shook her head.

"Look, I work in the newspaper business. Do you know how many journalists plan to write the great American novel? All of them. And do you know how many of them do? Very few, and only a small, small percentage of them ever get published.

"You've studied your field, and you know what you're doing—no illusions. You've got eight books, you tell me. Maybe it'll be your ninth or maybe your fourteenth, but it's got to happen for you. It's what you do. It's who you are." Sam took a big swallow of wine and replaced the glass on the table.

She could have kissed him. She wanted to kiss him. She took another drink of wine, waited for it to hit her stomach in one big burn, set her glass on the table next to his, and leaned forward to kiss the corner of his mouth.

Sam's arm dropped behind her, drawing her close against the tight muscles of his chest. He turned his head and reached for her chin with his hand, drawing her mouth in line with his own and outlining her lips gently with little kisses—and stirring feelings she had long thought she could live without. He stopped and drew back, watching her in the soft light.

"What is it?" she asked.

"Nothing."

"Tell me," she whispered.

"Where's the pod?"

She stared at him. She knew exactly what he meant, the crumb. She'd seen all the versions of *Invasion of the Body Snatchers*, including a few of the ripoffs.

For just a moment she'd thought she had him. Why couldn't he just accept her as a sultry, sexy seductress? Stupid question.

"No pods," she said, his face still close enough to hers to feel his breath on her cheek.

"And I guess you expect me to trust you, a pod-person. You're just waiting for me to go to sleep, aren't you, so that a pod can form into the shape of my body and take over."

Go to sleep—yes. And, at that point, a pod-person, a *cooperative* pod-person, would have been an improvement. She bit back all the smart retorts coursing through her mind, but she couldn't contain herself if she sat there one more second. She had to convince Sam, at least for the moment, that she wasn't at all like she really was.

Jennifer stood up, still holding his hand, and pulled him to his feet. "We need to eat," she said.

Sam wrapped his arms around her. "I already ate something," he said, folding her to him.

"Well, I didn't," she insisted, ducking back out of his hold, fully expecting to see sparks fly in the dim light.

What was she doing? She couldn't run away. Sam had to be convinced she'd let him spend the night with her. She turned back toward him, feeling like a yo-yo, not knowing which way to bob.

Sam must have seen the crazed look in her eyes. "Are you all right?" he asked.

Her plastic smile was back in place. "Fine. Perfect. It's just that I worked really hard on this supper and I want you to enjoy it. And I'm starved. Really, really hungry, and I get a little crazy when I haven't had anything to eat."

Sam scooped up his wineglass and drained it. "Next time, let me bring the wine. This stuff's a little bitter. Want me to help? I'm not a bad cook."

Jennifer stared at the empty glass as Sam put it back down. *Just don't let it hurt him,* she prayed.

"No, the salads are all ready. Just have a seat."

Jennifer placed the fresh, sliced bread on a small plate and put it between the place settings on the table. She scooped the two bowls of greens from the refrigerator, peeled back the plastic wrap, and sprinkled each with croutons and Parmesan cheese. "I do my own salad dressing. I hope you like it," she added, setting the bowl down in front of him and taking her seat.

Sam attacked the bowl with relish.

"I thought you weren't hungry," Jennifer said, watching his greedy descent into the food.

"I never said that. I said I'd already eaten—lunch. Besides, I had something else on my mind. Still do. But the salad will do for the time being." He picked up a piece of bread, tore it in two, and paused.

"What's wrong?" Jennifer asked.

"I don't know. I'm feeling a little spacey all of a sudden." He smiled a crooked smile. "Don't worry about me. I'll be all right."

No one was all right with ground-up sleeping pills and a full glass of wine in his stomach.

"Would you mind getting me another glass of wine?"

"Can't do it."

"What?"

"I only bought one bottle, and . . . and I want to save the rest to go with our dessert."

"Dessert?" His grin was getting more and more lopsided.

"Cheesecake with a thin chocolate sauce."

Sam's eyes drifted shut and then popped open. "Could you excuse me a minute?"

"Sure. What's the matter?"

Sam stood up. "I don't know. It's been a long week and I guess I'm simply exhausted. Maybe if I splash some water on my face."

He took an unsteady step back from the table.

Jennifer ducked under his arm and steadied him. "Let me help you," she offered. "I think you ought to lie down."

She steered him down the short hallway and pushed open the bedroom door. Muffy was all over them, panting and licking. She should have stashed her in the bathroom, but it was too small and the dog had a habit of jumping into and out of the bathtub, creating a ringing sound like one of those huge, old bells on some boat. Most distracting.

"Down, Muffy," Jennifer ordered, fruitlessly. Muffy only obeyed when Jennifer's hands weren't full. She was smart like that.

"Ice cream, Muffy, ice cream," Jennifer offered. The dog scrambled out of the room, and Jennifer managed to kick the door shut with her foot.

"What was that?" Sam slurred.

"My roommate. Let me get you down on the bed."

Sam was growing heavier. Jennifer shifted his weight and grabbed the comforter and top sheet with her free hand, pulling it awkwardly to the foot of the bed. Then she eased him onto the mattress. She wanted those covers down so she wouldn't be stuck trying to pull them out from under him after he passed out.

His head hit the pillow and he ran his hand absently over his face. "I'll be all right in a minute," he assured her. "I just need some time to relax."

She unlaced his shoes, dropped them next to the bed, and scooted his feet under the covers. As she reached for his tie, Sam grabbed her hand and pulled her down to him.

"I never thought . . ." he began. He kissed her full on the mouth, a long, passionate kiss that left Jennifer gasping. She drew back and sucked in a lungful of air. She hadn't been kissed with that much passion since Danny Buckner got her alone in his dad's old Chevrolet the night of their senior prom. But there was a major difference between Danny's needy, greedy, got-to-have-it kind of kiss and Sam's soulful, intoxicating . . .

She stood up.

"Don't," he pleaded. "Don't pull away." He still held her hand.

She knelt down next to the bed, resting her cheek

against his. "I haven't felt this way about anybody. . . ." His speech was becoming more and more indistinct. "Jennifer . . . Jennifer . . . I think I . . ." His breathing steadied, his eyes fell shut, and his fingers loosened around Jennifer's wrist.

And for one fleeting second she would have traded all possibility of fame and fortune just to hear the rest of Sam's sentence.

Chapter 22

Atlanta was a nightmare. Everybody in the city must have run out of food at the same time because they all had come out for a late supper and were thronging the restaurants on either side of O'Hara's Tara.

Jennifer pulled the oversized cardigan close around her as she pushed her way through the masses. The sweater was too loose to offer much protection from the cool, evening air, but she couldn't wear a Jennifer Marsh coat. It wouldn't be fair. She was in disguise, just as a real killer would be. She was Sophie—an unwed, pregnant, visually impaired waif and Mrs. Walker's latest adoptee.

Her mind wandered to her bedroom in Macon where she'd left Sam in a deep, sonorous sleep. She'd stayed longer than she had intended, watching over him, making sure his breathing was strong.

But she couldn't think about Sam right now. She was a woman on a mission, and nothing—*nothing and no one*—was going to distract her. She had to see if her plan would work, if she could pull it off, if she could actually get as far as Penney Richmond's door and then somehow get her to open it.

The reading glasses slid a little farther down her nose, and she silently cursed as she jammed them back into place. She'd have to make a mental note: all villains using glasses as a disguise had to have plain glass for lenses even if they had to run the risk of special-ordering them. She could barely see.

She adjusted the tote bag slung against her hip. Her dad's old revolver was inside, wrapped carefully in a soft cotton T-shirt. Six bullets were packed next to it folded into the toe of a sock. She assumed they went with the gun although she'd never actually tried to load it. Not that it mattered. If she were really going to shoot Penney Richmond, she'd probably need a silver bullet to keep her down. The woman was *not* a nice person.

Ernie held the door as Jennifer ducked into O'Hara's Tara.

"In to see your aunt?" he asked after her. "She forgot to tell me you were coming."

Jennifer put her finger over her mouth in a silent shhhh. She wanted to shush him loudly, to order him out of her way, not to deal with him at all. But Ernie wasn't going anywhere, and causing a scene was the last thing she wanted.

"I didn't tell her I was coming," Jennifer said. "It's a surprise."

"Oh, yeah? What's the occasion?"

Occasion? Did a person have to have an *occasion* to surprise someone? And since when did doormen have to get so involved in their tenants' lives?

"Uh . . ." Jennifer searched her mind. "Tiger's birthday."

"Ya don't say. I didn't think that little mutt had birthdays. Just between you and me, I thought maybe he was cooked up in some lab. Whatcha got in the bag?"

Jennifer felt the heat rise in her cheeks. "A doggie cake made out of rawhide," she fibbed.

Ernie's eyes narrowed, and Jennifer prayed he wouldn't ask to see it.

"It's got these cute little candlelike things that stick up from the center and the lacing looks like part of the icing." She was talking too much, far too much. She clamped her mouth shut.

"Yeah? They make stuff like that? You need help getting it up the stairs? It looks a little heavy." His eyes were focused on the bag's heavy droop.

Jennifer cupped the bottom of the tote and grinned foolishly. "Oh, that. That's the . . . pickles."

"Pickles?"

"Tiger loves pickles." She should have opted for something more believable—like a shrunken head.

Ernie chuckled. "So it's Tiger, is it, that loves pickles?" he said, pointedly staring at the bulge that her towel made under her misshapen dress. If she showed up in that getup one more time, Ernie would be taking up a collection to get her a new wardrobe. Fortunately, she wouldn't be coming back to O'Hara's Tara, at least not as pregnant Sophie.

"Whatever," Ernie was saying. "You have yourself a nice visit with your aunt. And if you get any twinges, you just let old Ernie know. I'll see you get the care you need."

Jennifer practically ran to the elevator. She pressed the button for the eleventh floor and waited for the doors to close. Then she took a tissue from her sweater pocket and wiped the panel clean. Even the most inexperienced murderer knew better than to leave fingerprints.

The doors opened and she stared at a young, well-dressed couple waiting in the hall. She pulled a few strands of the coarse, black wig across her face as she traded places with them, but she needn't have bothered. The woman's stare held a horrified look that seemed glued to Jennifer's misshapen clothes, and the man's only interest was in the slinky evening dress of his companion.

Why couldn't she have invented a persona that allowed her to wear dresses like that? That character would have been so much more fun to impersonate. Jolene Arizona would be in a long, blonde wig, a short sequined gown (to show off her legs), and dripping with rhinestones. Her name would be something exotic like Babette DuBois—not Sophie McClanahan. And inside her bra would be a tiny, jewel-handled, single-shot derringer. Of course, she'd have to contend with Ernie because she would have slept with him, and he'd be so enthralled with her that he could hardly let her get past the entranceway without . . . The Sophie persona was looking better and better.

"I'm calling the management first thing in the morning. Some of the people Ernie lets—" the woman was saying as the doors thumped shut.

Mercifully, the hallway was empty. Now if she could only find apartment 1129 and somehow get Penney Richmond to speak to her. That's all she needed, like touching base in a game of tag. If that door came open, it would be proof her plan had worked.

Jennifer walked the full length of the corridor, but she couldn't find any number over 1115. And then she remembered: Mrs. Walker had said something about Penney Richmond's apartment being in the other section of the building.

Jennifer trudged back to the elevator bank, pushed the *down* button, and slipped inside when the doors parted. Real-life murder—even a walk-through—was far more complicated than the stab'em, shoot'em, choke'em-from-behind stuff she wrote. Actually, she hardly ever wrote the murders. They had already happened before the book opened or they occurred neatly offstage somewhere. She'd never given much thought to how difficult it was.

For the first time since she'd started writing, she was beginning to feel sympathy for her villains, especially Marcus, that disgusting creature who heard voices whenever he opened his refrigerator. (A great argument for ordering takeout.) The man had an overwhelming task coming up with a dead body every month. He must have worked hard at it.

The elevator popped open on the ground floor, and a clown in full makeup with a curly rainbow-colored wig, a billowing polka-dotted costume, and a half-dozen balloons pushed past her. Too bad Miss Slinky Evening Gown missed that one.

Jennifer snuck across to the other bank of elevators. Fortunately, Ernie was well out of sight.

The elevator doors opened and a bevy of black-clad yuppies spilled forth. They seemed to be all together and far more intent on where they were going than on noticing some frump. She sighed her relief, stepped inside, and pounded the *eleven* button with the side of her fist. Within two minutes she was staring at the door to apartment 1129. Somewhere behind it, in the bowels of Penney's lair, was the dragon lady herself.

A ball of panic began to rise from her stomach and inch up her esophagus. One hand flew to her belly and the other to her mouth. Oh, great! All she had to do was be sick all over the carpet. She swallowed hard and kept up those short, little gulps that had worked to keep her steady in the past. Some of the nausea began to pass, but the electric charges that scampered through her muscles left her in no better shape.

How did real-life murderers do it? Just the thought of looking Penney Richmond in the eye had her digestive system in somersaults. She had to get away from the door.

She slunk down the hall and pulled open the fire door to the stairwell. She slumped onto the top stair and pulled her bag into her lap, the towel bunching at her waist, the towel that shouldn't be a towel at all, but Jaimie growing, thriving, comfortably happy in his/her mother's belly. Sweet little Jaimie, her confidant, her legacy, her future.

"Everything is all right," she whispered, foolishly patting the stupid towel. What did she think she was doing slinking around some woman's apartment building, stalking her like some lunatic? And for what? Research for some book?

She needed to get a grip. Why had she ever thought walking through some idiotic plan would give her some secret element that would finally make her books sell? Was that *all* she wanted out of life?

She'd left poor Sam drugged and sleeping for this? Sam didn't deserve what she'd done to him—nobody did, but especially not him. He believed in her. "It'll happen for you," he'd said, and he had meant it—and that was before the drugs hit his system.

And Jaimie would happen for her, too. Isn't that what Dee Dee had said, if only she'd give some poor guy a chance, some silly, dark-blue-eyed guy who just might be different from the Steve Moores of the world, who just might share her dreams with her?

Jennifer let out the breath she'd been holding. She wanted to be published more than almost anything in this world, but this charade was not the way to do it. She'd never know how a murderer felt. She couldn't conceive of it.

No more tricks or games or gimmicks. She'd write like she always had, tell the stories *she* wanted to tell. And she'd wait, wait to be discovered like everybody else. She'd go down to the post office first thing Monday morning, buy a roll of stamps, and create a postal blizzard with her queries. Somewhere out there was an agent who would someday see the value of her work.

She stood, readjusted her "baby," tugged open the heavy door to the hall, and ran to the elevator. She couldn't get out of the building fast enough. She wanted to be back in her own apartment, out of her Sophie clothes, making sure Sam was all right. She'd let him sleep through the night, make him a wonderful breakfast, tell him the whole ridiculous tale, and assure him nothing had happened between them—at least, not yet.

The elevator doors parted and the rainbow-wigged clown, still holding the balloons, stared at her in that eerie, unfriendly way that clowns have when they're not smiling. She stepped to one side, and the clown dragged his helium bouquet past her. She slipped into the elevator, pressed the *down* button, not caring this time if she left fingerprints, and breathed a sigh of relief as the compartment started to move. A freedom she hadn't felt in a long time washed over her. She had a lifetime to fulfill her dreams, and nothing was standing in her way.

Chapter 23

Someone was thumping on the door—loudly. Muffy was jumping up and down and skittering from the living room back into the bedroom, barking and snuffling. Jennifer groaned and rolled over in bed to stare through puffy, half-closed eyes at the clock on her bedside table. It read eight-fifty A.M. Way too early for someone to come visiting on a Saturday morning.

The building must be on fire was her first thought. She pulled the comforter up over her head and burrowed down. She'd dig out of the ashes later.

The thumping continued, only louder this time.

"Go away," she mumbled.

"Police. Open up."

Jennifer's eyes popped open and she dug her way out of the covers. What were the police doing at her door? And why wasn't Sam here? She could send him to get rid of them.

Last night she'd come home from Atlanta, dragging in close to two A.M. to find him gone, relieved that he was at least well enough to get himself up. They'd have plenty of time to discuss matters later. She might even find out what he'd been trying to say to her last night before he passed out.

She'd have to reconsider those mickeys she'd been slipping so casually in her books. They didn't always work.

"We know you're in there. Open the door."

The pounding continued. They must want someone down the hall, but it was becoming more and more obvious that the men in blue wouldn't leave until she opened the door.

She stumbled to the closet, grabbed a pair of jeans and a sweater, pulled them on, and headed to the door.

Another thought occurred to her. What if Sam had awakened, realized she'd drugged him, and gone to the police station to file a complaint against her? It was a few measly sleeping pills, for Heaven's sake, hardly enough—obviously—to do any real damage. She'd insist she was just trying to help him relax from all the stress of his work.

Jennifer paused at the door, took a deep breath, and released the lock. The door burst open. One plainclothes man and two uniformed officers, one male, one female, pushed their way in.

The detective, a big, burly, sandy-haired guy in a cheap gray suit, flashed his badge. She took it and inspected it. It belonged to Frank Sweeney of the Atlanta Police Department.

"You Jennifer Marsh?" Sweeney demanded.

"Yes," she said hesitantly. So much for the felon down the hall.

"Do you know a Penelope A. Richmond of Atlanta?"

A lump the size of a tennis ball formed around Jennifer's windpipe. Had Penney been watching through her peephole while she stood outside her door? Had she used some kind of alien, X-ray vision to pierce the cloth of her tote bag and see the gun she'd been carrying, and was

Penney now somehow accusing her of stalking? No wonder she had eight novels on her closet shelf. The man had asked her only one question and she already had enough material for three chapters.

"Do you know her?" the policeman repeated.

She cleared her throat and sucked in air. "Not personally. I know *of* her."

"Penelope Richmond received a number of threatening letters over the past two weeks, one of which was written on personalized stationery bearing your name and address and carrying what appears to be your signature. Several of the others are in the same handwriting. Do you know anything about that?"

So that was what this was about. Inwardly, Jennifer sighed her relief. At least she wasn't losing her mind. That creature Penney Richmond had reported her to the police for sending threats. Couldn't ol' Penney take a little joke?

"Oh, that." Jennifer shrugged. Maxie would be cool—ever so cool. "Samples from a book I wanted her to consider handling. You see, I'm a mystery writer and the letters are from a novel with this really screwed up villain named Marcus who—"

"Oh, yeah? Sounded like you thought this Richmond woman was some kind of Ebola virus."

Sweeney wasn't far off.

"Want to tell me where you were last night?" Sweeney asked.

Oh, sure. Why not? I was standing outside Penney Richmond's apartment trying to get up the nerve to con her into opening the door, so I could see what it's like to plan a murder.

Jennifer smiled sweetly. If she'd learned only one

thing from researching crime novels, it was not to answer any questions from a policeman, innocent or not, especially if she had no idea why he was asking them.

Muffy was still scampering around the room, rushing from one policeman to the next, rolling in front of them, begging to be petted. The traitor.

"Are you arresting me?" Jennifer asked. "You haven't read me my rights."

Muffy suddenly darted past Jennifer into the bedroom and came back shaking something black and hairy in her mouth.

"What's this?" Sweeney asked, bending and coaxing Muffy over to rub her back and extract the wig. He stood up, holding it in his hand. "What was that description we got from Ernest Tuttle?"

"You mean the doorman?" one of the uniforms asked.

"Yeah. Read me the one with the wig."

"He said she was young, in her twenties, pregnant, with large glasses and a long, black, curly wig. Went by the name of Sophie McClanahan."

Jennifer could feel the blood drain from her face. Whatever the police were there for, it was more than the threats. It had something to do with her being at O'Hara's Tara. But what?

"Said she was always wearing some god-awful brown floral dress and shapeless sweater. He thought she might be undergoing some kind of medical treatments that made her hair fall out because the three times he saw her, she was wearing the wig."

"Mind if we take a look in the bedroom?" Sweeney asked.

"You got a search warrant?" Jennifer silently prayed

that Muffy wouldn't drag out the Sophie dress she'd left in a heap on the floor near the wig last night.

"Not yet."

"Get it," she said defiantly.

"So you want to play it that way, do you?" Sweeney said. "Fine with me. You have the right to remain silent. If you give up the right to remain silent, anything you say can and will be used against you in a court of law. You have—"

"What's the charge?" Jennifer asked.

"For starters, it's making threats, and I do have a warrant for your arrest. We'll see how long it takes us to work up to first degree murder. Cuff her," Sweeney ordered the uniform.

Jennifer's knees buckled. Fortunately, the policeman was holding her wrists. "Who died?" she squeaked out, already sure of the answer.

"Have you been following this conversation?" he asked.

"Not well," she admitted.

"You have the right to speak with an attorney and to have an attorney present during questioning. If you so desire . . ."

In her mind, Jennifer tried to sort out what had happened. Penney Richmond must have somehow got herself killed. But the police were here, at her apartment, arresting *her*, and Sam was who-knows-where. She had no alibi, she had no defense, and it was becoming painfully obvious she had no future. Something had gone terribly, terribly wrong with her plan.

Chapter 24

The jail cell was cold. Cold and gray and ugly. And all Jennifer wanted was to go home.

Things were alive in that cell. Fortunately, they weren't human, but she'd spotted a large, unidentified insect earlier, and Heaven knows what was lurking on the microbiotic level. She shuddered and sat up a little straighter, clutching her sweater closer about her shoulders.

She'd got herself into it this time. And now, not only God, but the Law was going to get her for it.

Bargaining with Him didn't seem particularly promising at this point. Too many necessary admissions. After all, she had planned the whole murder even if she hadn't intended to carry it out. And just her luck, Someone Up There, no doubt, had been taking notes.

She sighed. Crime was so much easier to cope with as words on a computer, words that could be moved, deleted, and retyped, but this real life cement floor, iron bars, and (she couldn't force herself to look at it) that awful stainless steel toilet lurking in the corner, were more reality than she had ever hoped to deal with. She'd like to delete *that* thing with a keystroke.

She rubbed at the black ink on her fingertips. It marked her as the common criminal she was. It'd take a week for the stain to fade, not that it mattered. No telling how long she'd be locked up in the slammer. She'd been charged with communicating threats. Thank goodness she'd had enough sense to use a courier service so they couldn't charge her with a felony. Of course, if they could establish a link between her and the other poison pen letters— the ones she didn't write—they'd throw away the key to her cell, with or without the murder charge. They were mailed.

The judge had been reasonable in setting bail, if $10,000 could be considered reasonable. But then she hadn't looked the least bit threatening when she stood before him, scared witless.

Jennifer sank back against the wall. Where the heck was Dee Dee? She'd called her more than three hours ago. How long did it take to scare up a thousand dollars on a Saturday and get herself to Atlanta, anyway?

She sighed and let her eyes drift shut. Sam. If only she'd stayed with him at her apartment instead of forging ahead with her crazy plan. If only she'd recognized her feelings for him sooner. She would have, too, if it hadn't been for her outrageous ambition. Well, maybe she would have. She'd like to think she would have. If only she could be content with a normal life like everybody else. If only . . .

"Where'd you go?" a voice asked, the words drifting slowly into her consciousness.

"Sam," she murmured softly, turning her head to find a more comfortable position against the cinder-block wall. Sam had a wonderful, soothing voice, a voice that could lull her into thinking everything would be all right. A voice she could listen to . . .

"Where'd you go?" the voice asked again, this time suspiciously like a real, earthly, male voice.

Jennifer opened her eyes. It was Sam all right, and he was staring so intently at her she felt like she'd been doused with a bucket of ice water. She sat up, glad to have the bars between them.

"Sam?" she asked tentatively. "How did—"

"Dee Dee called me and asked me to get over here. You've got her scared half out of her mind. Her husband is out, and she didn't want to bring her little girl up here."

If Dee Dee couldn't come, why hadn't she just said so or called somebody—anybody—else? How could she deliver Jennifer into the hands of . . . of the very irritated man she'd drugged and left sleeping in her bed, a man who, at the moment, looked far too angry to be confused with a knight in shining armor.

"Are you ready to get out of here?"

Jennifer nodded numbly.

Sweeney and a police officer walked up behind Sam. The officer unlocked the cell and pulled open the door.

"You can go for now, but don't go far. I'll be in touch," Sweeney promised.

"What the hell were you thinking?" Sam asked as he eased his Honda onto I-75 south.

"Obviously I wasn't thinking, okay?" Jennifer slumped farther into the leather of the bucket seat, wishing she were anywhere else. Well, not anywhere. Sam's car was a step up from the jail cell. Too bad he went with it.

"Did you kill that woman?"

She stared at him with an open mouth. "I can't believe you felt you had to ask me that question. How *could* you?"

"How could *I*? How could *I*?"

At the moment, she wasn't up to a pronoun war. She turned and burrowed down into the seat's upholstery. She was exhausted, and she was scared. She closed her eyes and prayed that everything would go away—beginning with Sam.

She felt the car slow and opened her eyes to see that he had pulled onto the off ramp at a rest area.

He cut the motor and turned to her. "Talk to me, Jennifer," he said gently.

So he was changing tactics. He'd dropped the rough, tell-me-or-else attitude and was now trying the you-can-trust-me routine. As if she hadn't majored in psychology, not to mention being an expert on the good-cop, bad-cop routine. Hah! But she was trapped, too far out of Atlanta to walk back, and miles from Macon. There wasn't any getting away now. She took a deep breath and turned to face him.

"What do *you* think?" she asked, her chin stuck out.

"I think you're almost crazy enough to kill someone, but not quite. But you were up to something last night and I want to know what. And I want to know what you put in that wine you gave me. I woke up feeling queasy and barely made it to the bathroom before I got sick. By the way, that mutt of yours kept jumping into and out of the bathtub, making it ring like some death knell. Didn't help my head, either."

"Muffy has a habit of doing that when she's upset. Usually she stays out of the powder room unless I lock her in there or I'm sick or she's sick or—"

Sam let out a heavy sigh. "This Penelope Richmond—she was that woman at Steve Moore's party, the one who had you seeing red, the woman in teal."

Jennifer nodded.

"A literary agent?"

Again she nodded.

"You didn't kill her because of something she said to you that night, did you?"

Jennifer shook her head.

"Just checking. The police can place you at her apartment building close to the time of the murder. They searched your place and found some kind of outfit that the doorman identified."

"You must have good friends at the police department."

"I do—have to in my business. But they can't place you inside, at least not yet."

"That's because I wasn't there. I never got in. I never even tried." Her voice cracked and a small tear traced a path down her cheek.

"What's this all about?" Sam asked quietly. He reached over and took her hand in his.

"It's all Oprah's fault," she blurted, the tears flowing freely now for the first time. "She had this woman on her show who had written this book . . ." and she told Sam the whole story from beginning to end, leaving out only a few irrelevant, personal details about him.

"And you planned that whole scene last night with me at your apartment because . . ."

"I wanted to see if a man would believe he had spent the night making love to a woman even if he woke in the morning and couldn't remember anything. I needed to know if he would think the woman had been there with him all night. That's what the evening was supposed to be, but that's not how it turned out."

"Because I woke up and left."

"No, you idiot, because of what happened between

us." Jennifer groaned and wiped her face with the back of her hand. "I know how stupid this all sounds. I'm totally neurotic and hopelessly out of touch with my feelings. Haven't you figured that out yet?"

"The neurotic part had not eluded me."

She turned away and looked out the car window. "I actually had thought about killing Penney Richmond, and now I'm being punished for it. You have every right to throw me out of your car right now. I don't blame you for believing I killed her," she said softly.

She felt herself being pulled backward, turned and then folded into Sam's arms, cradled firmly against his chest, the emergency brake sticking painfully into her abdomen.

And then she heard him start to chuckle and then to laugh. How could he? She tried to pull away, but he held her tight against him.

"Ah, Jennifer. You couldn't have killed that woman if she'd cocked the gun for you, pinned a bull's-eye over her heart, and begged you to shoot her."

He stroked her hair, and she relaxed as best she could, considering the brake.

"Part of your crazy scheme worked perfectly," he said. "The part to make you the prime suspect. We've got our work cut out for us. Unless we find out who the murderer is, there's a real possibility you're going to be spending the next twenty years of your life in jail."

Chapter 25

The tears were gone, and the adrenaline—the good kind—had kicked in big-time. Jennifer's mind was as sharp as she ever dreamed Maxie Malone's could be, at least on a Saturday night after spending most of the day in jail. So why, with a super dose of sleuthing hormones racing through her, didn't she have a clue how to start solving the puzzle of Penney Richmond's death?

A murderer—the bad kind, the kind who actually killed people—was loose out there somewhere, and she was being blamed. And it looked as though the police would be content to let her fry. She couldn't blame them. After all, she'd planned it that way, planned that the police would have no choice but to see her as their only suspect. Success. Why did it have to be so selective?

Jennifer stared at the blank tablet that lay on her dining table. Two sharpened number-two pencils lay idle beside it. This was as hard as staring at the first, blank page of a novel, hoping something, anything, would somehow magically appear, like lemon-juice writing brought near a flame.

Muffy shifted near her feet and rested her chin possessively on the toe of Jennifer's shoe. Since she'd come home, Muffy hadn't let her get more than a few feet away.

"Drink this," Sam ordered, coming in from the kitchen nook and plopping down a big mug of steaming coffee.

She grabbed it up and took a big swallow, burning off most of her taste buds in one fell swoop.

"Careful. It's hot," Sam warned.

She nodded, her tongue swelling. She was not about to complain. Sam had come to her rescue, brought her home, and fed her a cheese omelet. This could be true love.

She liked the way he looked, rather domestic with his tie off, his sleeves rolled up, and a dusting of toast flakes dotting his white shirt.

"Come up with anything yet?"

"Only that Penney Richmond received more threats than the ones I sent. They all came in envelopes with Macon postmarks."

"Then our murderer is right here," Sam concluded.

Jennifer screwed up her face and took another scalding gulp of coffee. "Not necessarily. *I* made threats but *I* didn't kill her."

"You have . . . unusual thought processes."

Jennifer shrugged. It didn't matter. She had to follow the threats. They were the only lead she had.

"I don't know how the police think I could have written those other notes."

"Did they present them before the judge when you were charged?"

Jennifer nodded. "The whole M.O. was different: printed, not handwritten, on plain paper, sent through the mail, and the wording . . . the wording was so unimaginative."

"What'd they say? Do you remember?"

"Something like, 'You know what you did. How can you sleep at night? You'll never hurt anyone else again.'

B-movie stuff like that. A whole different style from Marcus's classic, Poe-esque ramblings."

Sam yawned. "Right. So where do we start?"

Suddenly it seemed so obvious. No wonder Sherlock Holmes kept Dr. Watson around to ask the questions, to force an answer. And the answer was as logical as any synopsis she'd ever put together. Maxie Malone always started her investigations by running down the victim's associates and by visiting the crime scene.

"Two places: Steve Moore's guest list for his party, and O'Hara's Tara. I assume most of Penney's Macon clients would have been invited."

"That's assuming it was a client that killed her."

"I'm not assuming anything, but I'm sure most of them had motive, and we've got to start somewhere."

"And the apartment building?"

"I wasn't the only one at O'Hara's Tara that night. The place was teeming with people, and one of them had to be the murderer, unless Penney got wind of my plan and committed suicide just to frame me. She wasn't a very nice person, you know."

"So I've been told. How do we get a copy of Moore's guest list?"

"It's got to be in his office. I'm sure Edith was involved in planning that party. Moore couldn't tie his shoelaces by himself."

"You can't go back to Channel 14. Sunday's paper will carry an article about your arrest. By the way, you do have a good publicity photo, don't you? If not, we'll have to lift one from your high school yearbook."

Betrayal had a name, and it was Sam Culpepper. "*We?* Tell me you didn't—"

"The *Telegraph* can't ignore a story like this one, you

know that. But I did some fairly clever damage control. I led off with a paragraph about your writing—"

"You 'led off'?"

Anger was not an appropriate reaction. Jennifer kept telling herself that, but the shudder that threatened to radiate from her gut wasn't asking for intellectual approval.

Suddenly her brain intervened with a scary flash of realization. Just as she'd anticipated in her demented, murderous planning stage, she was going to get some publicity out of Penney Richmond's murder. That publicity, thanks to her connection with Sam, was going to center around an aspiring novelist, not a caterer. And if she helped him, she just might come out of this mess with some part of her reputation intact. Not that anyone had heard of her, but she'd been brought up to believe she could survive almost anything as long as she kept her dignity.

"I'll get you that photo before you leave. I had it taken last year when an editor almost bought the first Maxie Malone book. I keep it in what I call my hope chest, along with a bio and some possible blurbs for book jackets. You can have those, too, if you want."

"I do. Now, how are we going to get into Moore's office?"

"Moore and Allen were using a temp company before he hired me. I overheard Edith on the phone with them the day I was hired. What if a rep calls Monday morning saying a replacement is on the way over?"

"Not the wig again."

Jennifer tried to stick out her swollen tongue. "Are you kidding? The police kept it as evidence. I'll send Teri. She's off Mondays, and she's great with computers."

"Who's Teri, and can she pull something like this off?"

"She writes romantic intrigue. She'll do great."

"What if Moore's secretary recognizes your voice?"

"Edith doesn't come in until nine. I'll speak to the front desk receptionist and have her leave a note. Edith usually has two or three messages waiting for her each morning."

"And O'Hara's Tara?"

"That one I'll have to deal with myself. Mrs. Walker deserves an explanation. I wouldn't be surprised to find she'd set up a college fund for 'our little one,' a.k.a. my towel."

"She's sending your towel to college?"

"It was a complicated relationship."

Sam nodded knowingly. "Will they let you back into the building?"

"The judge didn't issue a restraining order, so I don't see why not. We'll try first thing tomorrow morning."

The Sunday paper lay crumpled between the bucket seats of the Accord.

"It's a long way to Atlanta—about eighty miles. Don't tell me you don't plan to talk to me the whole hour and a half it'll take us to get there." Sam had tried cajoling, joking, and a sterner, no-nonsense approach. Now he was back to coaxing.

Jennifer continued to stare out the car window. How could he? How could he let them put that awful, terrible, no-good headline over her lovely photo? It had been shot through a soft filter, in black and white, one slender hand supporting the side of her face, a half smile on her lips, her hair curled softly in a kind of Forties glamour look. And over the top of that picture were supposed to be the

words: LOCAL AUTHOR ASTOUNDS CRITICS BY ACHIEV-
ING NEW YORK TIMES BESTSELLER LIST WITH FIRST
NOVEL. Instead, the headline read: MACON WOMAN IN-
DICTED FOR THREATENING MURDER VICTIM.

"I don't write the headlines. I told you that. I was
lucky to get the article past the editor without any major
revisions. Besides, it's not a bad headline. It doesn't say
'Mystery Novelist Suspected of Having Lived out Murderous Fantasy' or 'Bitter Writer Takes Revenge on Literary Agent.' "

Jennifer wondered if Sam realized how truly futile his
lame, insensitive attempts to get her to talk really were.
Under the circumstances, she wished he would show
some maturity and just accept her decision to pretend he
didn't exist. Besides, despite what he continued to say
with almost every combination of words possible—she'd
been admiring his ingenuity for the last fifteen miles—
she doubted he really wanted to hear how she felt.

"Did you read the fourth paragraph? I got in two of the
titles of your books, and I was even able to slip in a brief
synopsis of your new Jolene Arizona novel."

He would pick that one. Any juror who got wind of Jolene's exploits would put her creator in jail on both literary and moral grounds. And justly so for the sheer act of
devising that plot.

Jennifer had hoped to make a scrapbook for little
Jaimie, detailing his/her mother's success before her/his—
dang this gender nonsense—birth. Clippings from local
and not-so-local newspapers, proclaiming her achieve-
ments, her honors, her—

"Jennifer, this has got to stop."

Now he was taking a paternal stance. She hated that

tone of voice even when her own father had used it. He was recycling, running out of ways to force a response. But then all languages, she supposed, had their limits.

"Look. I did my best for you. I really did and if—"

"Thank you." The words surprised Jennifer almost as much as they did Sam, who had to swerve to recover his lane.

Sam was trying. He really was, and she knew that. Yesterday evening she thought she had her feelings under control, that she was going to be able to deal with having her name and image splashed across the media. And she'd continued to think so right up until she saw the article, in real black ink on flimsy newspaper stock, right up until the moment it had become tangible—and delivered to almost every doorstep in the Macon area. Shame. It was such a Southern emotion.

Jennifer had yet to count her allies, and she realized with her last shred of rationality that if she were going to keep Sam, she'd better get with it.

She'd seen Dee Dee only briefly when she dropped off Muffy, and she hadn't spoken to any of her critique group. They wouldn't know about her arrest until they read the paper this morning. She hoped her answering machine was accumulating their words of support even as she and Sam sped toward Atlanta. But one never knew. Friends were unpredictable. They must be tested to know which ones stand strong and which ones disappear at the first hint of trouble. And an accusation of murder was more than a *hint*.

Sam was her friend. He was practically begging to be her friend, and she'd been treating him like . . . well, with less respect than he deserved. She could count on him.

When they got to Atlanta in just a few minutes, she'd

find out about another important player in this drama, one who could help her or hurt her. Yes, there was a significant question to be answered at O'Hara's Tara. Whose friend was Mrs. Walker—Jennifer's or Sophie's?

Chapter 26

Ernie seemed more confused than suspicious as Jennifer watched his eyes travel up and down her slender frame, pausing on the flat of her stomach.

"No baby," he declared. He obviously felt betrayed. Jennifer was certain he'd hoped to deliver her baby and suspected he might even have hoped to eke out a godfather spot in the process.

"Nope. Never was," Jennifer confessed.

"Is this the guy who wasn't the father?" he asked, gesturing at Sam.

Jennifer stared at him, not sure what to say.

"I like the hair better." Ernie nodded approvingly. "The color suits your complexion. And the clothes," he added.

"Ernie, just ring Mrs. Emma Walker for me."

"Your aunt?"

"No, she's not my aunt."

"And I guess the other night wasn't Tiger's birthday, either?"

"You were right. Tiger doesn't have birthdays. He's some kind of alien life-form. Just ring her."

"I don't know if I'm supposed to be doing this."

Jennifer smiled her best, trust-me-I-know-what-I'm-doing smile. "What instructions did the police give you?"

"No one is to go into Ms. Richmond's apartment without their permission."

"Was that it?"

Ernie nodded.

"So, you see, it's just fine if I go up to see Mrs. Walker. Call her," Jennifer insisted.

Ernie hesitated.

"Please," she added, stifling an urge to create another crime scene.

Ernie took up the phone and turned his back on Jennifer and Sam, whispering into the receiver.

He turned again, and Jennifer once more felt that searching, intrusive study of her unpregnant self. "Are you sure?" he was saying. "If it was up to me . . . yeah. No. Okay. I understand, but I'll keep an ear out and if anything . . ." He lowered his voice and cupped the mouthpiece with his left hand. "Yes, I did like your Christmas bonus, Miz Walker . . . uh-huh. I do understand who pays my salary. I'll send them right up."

Ernie hung up the phone and cleared his throat.

"You can go on up. Mrs. Walker—she's in quite a state. Says she's been expecting you for two days."

Mrs. Walker desperately crushed Jennifer against her petite frame. "Where have you been?" she demanded. "I've been worried sick about you. Do you know there's been a murder in this building? But of course you do, the police arrested you for it—you, of all people."

Jennifer drew back and cocked an eyebrow.

"Get yourself and whoever this is that you've brought with you on into the living room," Mrs. Walker ordered, pushing Jennifer down the hall before shutting and locking the door. "Who knows what kind of lunatic may be roaming the halls. Now, why didn't you call me? I can't bear to think of you in that horrible police station. I would have sprung you, dear, surely you know that."

Sam obediently followed Jennifer to the sofa, where they sank into the downy cushions and Tiger nipped and snarled first at one shoe and then the next.

Mrs. Walker impatiently grabbed the beast and carried him down the hallway. Jennifer heard the door to the powder room slam shut. Mrs. Walker returned, breathless. "I love that critter, but sometimes I wish I'd left the little rat in the alley where I found him."

Mrs. Walker obviously mistook Jennifer's surprise for horror. "Oh, don't worry, dear. I'll let him out later. We can't very well have him chewing up your shoes, now can we?"

Suddenly, Mrs. Walker seemed to catch sight of Jennifer's flat abdomen. She let out a strangled shriek. "The baby! Don't tell me—"

"There never was a baby, Mrs. Walker. I'm sorry. I never meant to deceive you."

"Well, thank God for that. For a moment there I was afraid this mess had caused you to miscarry, but then I don't suppose it made your hair turn brown." Mrs. Walker leaned forward and carefully inspected Jennifer's tresses. "And straight, I might add."

"It was a wig," Jennifer explained.

"So the police told me when they came by yesterday afternoon. They brought it for me to identify." She laughed self-consciously. "My eyes aren't quite as good as they used to be, but then neither is the rest of me. They tried to grill me, but I wouldn't squeal. I insisted on serving them something to drink before I'd answer any questions, and then I plunked a tea bag in each cup and filled it with coffee." The old woman laughed devilishly. "They think I'm demented. They couldn't get out of here fast enough."

Jennifer took a deep breath. "You've got a right to know who I really am. My name isn't Sophie. It's Jennifer, Jennifer Marsh, and I'm not Italian."

"Of course you're not. I can see that perfectly well now, and that horrible mug shot they showed me hardly did you justice."

Mrs. Walker again leaned forward and said in a hushed voice, "Now give me the lowdown. Were you on a stakeout? Do you work for some gumshoe? And who's the hunk you've got in tow?"

Sam reached past Jennifer and shook Mrs. Walker's hand. "Sam Culpepper."

"Nice eyes. He your boss or some other operative?" Mrs. Walker gave Sam a good once-over out of the corner of her eyes.

"Macon Telegraph," Sam explained.

"A journalist. How nice." She beamed at Sam and then leaned to whisper into Jennifer's ear, "They don't make much money, you know."

"I know. Mrs. Walker, we need your help."

"Well, of course you do, dear. Why else would you be here?"

"Were you here Friday night when Ms. Richmond was murdered?" Sam asked.

"I was in the building. I got back to my place shortly after nine. Mae Belle had three of us in for a few hands

of bridge and a light supper. She's three floors down."
Mrs. Walker studied Jennifer's face. "Why did you come
here in the first place, dear, and get yourself in so much
trouble?"

Lying now seemed pathetic, even if the truth sounded
ridiculous.

"I was researching a mystery novel I want to write,"
Jennifer said.

"Oh, you're a novelist! I should have guessed. How
absolutely fabulous," Mrs. Walker squealed. "Have you
written anything I might have read?"

"Not unless you've been in my closet."

Mrs. Walker stared at her blankly.

"Actually, I'm not published yet," Jennifer rushed on.

Mrs. Walker patted her hand. "Someone as clever as
you, dear, should have no trouble. . . ."

Someone as clever as she should never have gotten
herself into a situation where she could be charged with
murder. But all that aside, she didn't have time to clue
Mrs. Walker in to the harsh realities of book publishing.

"The police think I killed Penney Richmond."

"Now why on earth would they believe that?"

Jennifer bowed her head. "I sort of wrote her a few
notes that could have been mistaken . . ."

"Oh, dear, dear. I think I understand. She was a literary
agent. Yes, I see now. Really, I'm surprised at you, Jennifer. Surely you know better than to put anything in
writing. I've always preferred using the telephone myself. That way there is no hard evidence—of the threats, I
mean, unless, of course, they have one of those answering machines with the *Record* feature, but generally they
give themselves away before they press the button. And

then so many people have caller ID now. A pay phone is really the best. Remember that for the future."

Sweet Mrs. Walker had more sides to her personality than Jennifer had imagined.

Sam curtailed the old woman's lesson plan in electronic harassment. "Whoever killed Richmond was in this building Friday night, sometime between nine and midnight."

"Yes, that would logically follow, wouldn't it," Mrs. Walker agreed.

"Do you think you could find out, ask around, if any of the tenants saw someone suspicious in the building that night? Maybe get your bridge friends to help," he continued.

"Sort of like Holmes's Baker Street Irregulars, you mean?"

"Exactly," Jennifer agreed.

"I see. My friends and I aren't exactly a band of street urchins, but I'll see what I can do. I suppose you'd like us to throw in whatever gossip we can manage to dig up, too."

Jennifer nodded vigorously. "Most definitely. Didn't you mention something about Penney Richmond having a lover?"

"She was fond of entertaining on Friday nights, or so I've been told, although I personally haven't seen anyone I thought was in to see her recently," Mrs. Walker said. "I assumed the gentleman who used to come regularly was her lover, but assuming for purposes of gossip and assuming for a murder investigation, I suppose, would be two separate things."

"Do you know what he looks like?"

"But of course, although I suppose *looked* like would be more appropriate. He was that incredibly handsome newsman—the one that took a dive off that building in Macon. Kyle Browning."

Chapter 27

"Get over here right now!" Teri insisted over the phone.

"What are you doing?" Jennifer demanded, balancing a spoonful of jelly in midair, dripping a little onto her kitchen counter. "I can't go to the Channel 14 studios. That's why I sent you, remember?" She dabbed a bit of the red goo in each of three thumbprint cookies resting on an aluminum baking pan atop her stove. "Besides, I've got two dozen more cookies to bake before Dee Dee picks them up at two o'clock."

"I don't care. I can't find that damn paper you wanted me to get and I'm not coming back tomorrow to get it! How many hands does that man have anyway?"

"I told you to watch out for Moore."

"Moore? Moore's a pussycat. I'm talking about that Allen dude."

John Allen was hitting on Teri? Adonislike John Allen who had never given her more than a bored, where's-my-mail stare?

"Allen's not supposed to be there until late," Jennifer argued.

"The best I can tell, he had some kind of meeting with the higher-ups at nine o'clock, but don't quote me. How the heck am I supposed to know what's going on? I'm not even a real temp."

"You don't have to know anything. All you have to do is find one lousy—"

"I mean it, Jennifer. Are you listening to me? You've got to come now. We don't have much time."

Jennifer dropped the spoon into the jelly jar and licked her finger. "I can't come at all, not with Moore, Allen, and Edith there. You are there for a reason. I am here for a reason. What part of this scenario don't you understand? And who's listening to this conversation, anyway?"

"No one. They're gone—all of them. Outta here. And that's what I'm going to be if you don't hop in your buggy and get your ornery self over here this minute."

"How'd you get rid of them?"

"Don't worry. I took care of it."

"Teri . . ."

"Okay. I sorta called the police anonymously and suggested that an officer might want to question them because you'd been working here last week."

"You what?"

"Don't have a hissy fit. It worked. The police called them in, and there's no one in the office now except for me. I told Edith not to worry, I'd cover. I've looked through everything I can think of, Jen. It'd sure help if I had a clue what I was looking for."

Teri could come up with a plan to evacuate a news office, but she couldn't find a simple party roster.

"It's a list of names—last name first—phone numbers, addresses . . ."

"You better make it quick," Teri warned. "It's almost ten-thirty, and you can bet the police will let at least Moore loose in time for his broadcast at noon."

She'd kill her! She would go to Channel 14 and kill Teri—strangle her with her bare hands. But then thoughts like that were what got her into this mess to begin with.

"Tell the receptionist you're my supervisor," Teri instructed. "I've already told her you'd be over in a few minutes to do my evaluation. Just get your skinny little self over here now."

Jennifer was going for a 1950s Lana Turner look, a scarf wrapped around her hair and neck, big, dark glasses shielding half her face, and lipstick the color of a fire engine. An oversized, calf-length, all-weather coat covered her from the neck down. She ducked down the hall and slipped into Moore's office.

Teri turned and stared at her openmouthed. "You look like Audrey Hepburn swallowed by a manatee. How'd you get past the receptionist?"

"She was flirting with the security guard. They didn't even notice me."

"Whoa-ho. They'd have to be in one serious clinch not to notice you."

Jennifer took a long look at Teri. She was dressed in a tight spandex top and a leather miniskirt that showed more of her bronze, athletic legs than should have been legally allowed. "Is that a really wide belt or what?"

"The tag said it was a skirt. Who am I to argue? Besides, I figured if I could keep the boss distracted, he might not be so suspicious."

Distracted? She was surprised Moore hadn't had a heart attack.

Jennifer tossed her purse onto her former desk. "We don't have much time. I've got cookies to bake and police to avoid. Where have you looked?"

"There." Teri pointed to the filing cabinet. "And I went through Moore's desk drawers. Unless he's got the list coded somehow, I don't think it's there."

"And Edith's desk?"

"I looked through some of it, but I didn't find anything. I wouldn't be surprised if she's rigged one of the drawers with explosives. That woman gives me the creeps."

"She's just efficient. You could learn something from her," Jennifer added under her breath.

She plunked herself down in Edith's chair, tossed off her dark glasses, and rifled through the desk drawer. Nothing there, just as Teri had said. She pulled open the small file drawer on the right side of the desk, extracted a handful of manila folders, and plopped them down in front of her. The third one down was labeled BOOK SIGN-INGS. Inside was a tentative schedule of times and places Steve Moore would be promoting his book when it came out. It must be the tour Moore had wanted her to join him on, she thought. The next page down was a list of names and addresses with a sticky label on top reminding Edith to send all the people on the list notification of local and Atlanta book signings. It was the names of the guests who attended the party Jennifer had catered.

"I found it," she called to Teri.

"Found what?" a voice demanded. Jennifer looked up to see Lily Dawber standing in the doorway.

Oh crud. Mrs. Adonis, looking her domineering best. Jennifer ducked her head and covered her eyes with the glasses. If only she had John Allen nearby to toss to the shark.

"Can I help you?" Teri asked, sashaying over to Dawber.

"Who *are* you two?"

Teri took Dawber by the elbow and steered her toward John's office. "Mrs. Allen, you just missed your husband. Wouldn't you like to wait for him?

"I have to tell you," Teri added, "how much I loved you in the Miss Georgia pageant. As far as I'm concerned you were robbed. You're a lot more talented than that gal who won. I mean not just anyone can sing and dance ballet at the same time. As a matter of fact, I'm not sure I've ever seen anyone—"

"Who are you?" Dawber repeated, extracting her elbow and rooting herself to the spot.

"Yasmine. Yasmine Simone, the new temp." Teri stuck out her hand.

"Yasmine?" Dawber took Teri's hand in one of those three-finger, what-kind-of-disease-comes-standard-with-that-miniskirt kind of grip. "How do you do?"

Thank goodness for Southern gentility. It almost always won out.

"So many of you young women are in and out of here, it's impossible to keep up. And who is she?" Dawber pointed at Jennifer as though she could neither see nor hear.

Jennifer turned away.

"Don't look," Teri warned, leaning in confidentially. "She's a witness in a murder case."

Dawber's eyes widened.

"Just seeing her can put you in danger. Steve Moore plans to question her in one of those shadow-type interviews on the noon news. No one is supposed to be in here."

"If she's that important, I don't see why they don't have John do the interview at six."

Maybe because John doesn't know how to string three words together, Jennifer thought.

"She'll be out of here way before that. Witness protection program," Teri explained. She opened Allen's door and shoved Dawber inside. "Wait here while I move the moll to a more secure location."

Teri shut the door on Dawber's gaping mouth.

"Come on. Let's blow this joint." Teri grabbed her purse and Jennifer's as Jennifer scooped up the book-signing file and shoved the rest back into the drawer.

They had barely cleared the doorway when they heard the ding of the elevator followed by the silky rich voice of Steve Moore. They turned and ran for the stairwell, slipping totally out of sight before Moore and whomever he was with appeared in the hallway.

"Moll?" Jennifer asked as they fled down the stairs. "You think I look like a moll?"

"I got us out of there, didn't I?"

"You sure did, Yasmine. And I don't suppose Moore is going to be at all suspicious when he finds Dawber in Allen's office babbling about some Mafia babe he's going to interview who's part of the witness protection program."

"Look, improvisation is not my strong point. I didn't hear *you* offering any explanations. We made it out—at least of the office—and no one knows who we are."

"Sure they do—Yasmine! Or at least they will when your book finally sells, Teri. And a gun moll, of all things. You think just like you write, you know that?"

They came to a landing with a door marked *1*.

"You check it out," Jennifer ordered.

Teri cracked the door and stuck her head out. "Come

on. The place is full of people. Looks like some kind of tour group."

Jennifer laid a hand on Teri's arm. "Two seconds." She stripped off the coat, laid it over her arm, pulled off the scarf, and raked her lips with a tissue.

"Good thinking," Teri agreed. "At least we won't look like 'Teri and her trained porpoise.' "

It was a group all right—of fifth grade children. Not the easiest crowd Jennifer had ever tried to blend in with. She put on her best teacher face and headed straight for the door.

They gulped in the fresh air of freedom and sprinted toward their cars in the visitors' section.

"Catch you tonight," Teri called.

Chapter 28

Jennifer's critique group was a kind of sisterhood wrought from common ambition and eternal rejection. They embraced her warmly into the fold. After all, what was a little suspicion of murder among friends?

"Think of all the firsthand experience you're getting," April declared. "It's got to be great research to actually be behind those bars, know what it feels like to be caged, to be unjustly accused and left to rot for someone else's crime."

Leave it to April to put the best light on a situation and then turn it into "The Pit and the Pendulum." She pulled a bunch of grapes from the lunch bag perched precariously on her ever expanding abdomen. "Anyone want some?" she offered.

Leigh Ann withdrew her size-five feet from under her and leaned forward from her seat on Monique's couch. "Tell me about all those rugged, good-looking policemen, Jennifer. Don't you just love it when they pull their hats down to their eyebrows and put on those mirrored, wire-rimmed glasses?" A little shudder visibly ran through her body. "All business, yet so mysterious. You stare into their faces, all the while never knowing what they're thinking, what they're feeling, what—"

"You're sick. You know that?" Teri declared from the spot where she was curled on the floor at Leigh Ann's feet. Thankfully, she had traded her "work clothes" for sweatpants and an oversized shirt.

Monique let out her standard gasp of exasperation. "Just how can we help, Jennifer?" she asked. "Actually, I'm surprised someone didn't kill Penney Richmond years ago."

Four pairs of eyes made a collective turn toward Monique, who suddenly looked incredibly uncomfortable, so unlike the self-assured rock-of-knowledge they were so accustomed to.

"You knew her, didn't you?" Jennifer asked.

"I've met her."

Jennifer studied the woman's face. "No. No, this is more than that. A lot of agents' names have come up during our meetings, but I don't recall you ever saying anything about Richmond."

"That's right, even when Jennifer came in here complaining what a witch the woman had been to her over the phone that time," Leigh Ann agreed, nodding enthusiastically.

"Yeah," Teri chimed in. "You usually have all kinds of comments whenever—"

"All right. You might as well know," Monique said. "It's not like it's a secret. Penney Richmond was the agent who sold my book."

Light dawned in April's eyes and she paused in mid-chew, tapping her bottom lip with a grape. "Oh, my . . . She screwed you over, didn't she?"

"Let's just say she helped me understand the concept of justifiable homicide." Monique lay back in her chair and slowly started rocking.

Well, well. Jennifer wasn't the only one with impure thoughts. She suddenly felt an unexpected rapport with Monique.

"You've told us this much. You might as well give us the whole story," Jennifer coaxed.

"After my novel was bought, I put together two detailed synopses, twenty or so pages each. Penney kept them for three months before tossing them back at me. She said another client had written a book so similar to one of my ideas that there was no way she or anybody else could sell it."

Until that moment, Jennifer had only suspected the true depths of Penney Richmond's despicable nature.

"You think she stole it," Jennifer concluded.

The rocking stopped, and an infusion of blood reddened Monique's face. "Of course she stole it. When the book came out, the alternate universe I had created was right there in print, only with a well-known author's name across the book cover. We had words. Richmond told me she was dropping me as a client. She needed someone with more *original* thoughts."

"Why didn't you sue?" April asked.

"Are you kidding? Do you know how hard it is to prove someone stole an idea? I might have had a chance if I'd completed the manuscript and if someone had actually read it. All I had was a synopsis, a synopsis that only two people had seen: myself and Penney Richmond. For all I know, the author who wrote the book never even saw my work. Penney could have fed it to him in a brainstorming session."

"Bummer," Teri observed.

A true career S.O.B. At least Jennifer had been right about Penney Richmond. Monique's once promising career had simply dried up and blown away. When her book came out, it did only modest sales and then faded into oblivion. Monique had suffered off and on from writer's block ever since, and only now did Jennifer understand why.

"But this mess isn't about me," Monique reminded the group. "It's about Jennifer. What are we going to do to help?"

"I've got a day's leave I need to take," Leigh Ann volunteered. "Teri and I could go to Atlanta and check out Richmond's agency."

"We'll find out who her associates are and who's on her staff," Teri agreed.

"If possible, see if you can find out when or if Kyle Browning ever sent Penney Richmond a complete manuscript," Jennifer said. "She would probably have gotten it sometime during a six-month period ending about four months ago."

"We'll do our best," Leigh Ann promised.

"I'll get on the phone with some of Richmond's clients and see if I can get the word on what she's been up to," Monique offered. "And I'll put out the word on the Internet. See if I can scare up any of her more recent stunts."

"Anything you come up with will be hard to prove if she was as clever as she seems," Jennifer pointed out.

"True," Teri replied. "But we're not out to prove anything, only muddy the waters a little, come up with some names to throw at the police."

"And I can help Dee Dee cook, so you'll have more time to investigate," April suggested, sucking on yet another grape.

April was a fabulous cook. She'd be a great help to Dee Dee—if she didn't sample too many of the wares.

Jennifer could feel her throat start to constrict and her eyes well with tears. God love 'em. These were her spiritual sisters. An attack against one was an attack against them all. They were closing ranks, and whether they produced something that would help exonerate her or nothing at all, they were solidly behind her and exactly what she needed.

Chapter 29

Atlanta was a long way to go for lunch, especially on a Tuesday morning, but Mrs. Walker had been adamant over the phone. She had to see Jennifer and Sam right away, in person. She refused to explain, citing all the latest surveillance equipment that, she assured Jennifer, could allow almost anyone to drop in on their conversation. Mrs. Walker sounded suspiciously like a CIA operative.

Wagner's *Ride of the Valkyrie* was playing loudly as Mrs. Walker opened the door and ushered Sam and Jennifer into the dining room. Two well-dressed, white-haired, grandmother types sat waiting for them.

"Won't you have a seat?" Mrs. Walker suggested, gesturing to two side chairs. A lunch of finger sandwiches and various salads was spread on the table.

Tiger was nowhere to be found, but between cymbal clashes Jennifer thought she could detect faint yips coming from the direction of the bedroom. The sounds were either yips or the vibrations of her eardrums.

"I don't suppose you could turn down the music just a bit?" Jennifer asked.

"I want you to hear this piece in all its glory," Mrs. Walker shouted enthusiastically over the din. The orchestra reached a crescendo only Wagner could score. Mrs. Walker leaned down between the pair and whispered, "They can't hear us with the music, you see."

They? Jennifer took a deep breath and asked, "Who might *they* be?"

"Police. The murderer. Who knows? Your life is at stake, dear, and we'll take no chances."

Sam was unsuccessfully suppressing a grin.

Jennifer let out the breath she'd been holding. At least Mrs. Walker's paranoid fantasies weren't specific. She'd half expected the woman to tell her about the little gray men, the ones that came for her in the night.

"I want you two to meet the girls, Mae Belle and Jessie."

Mae Belle was a little woman with a toothy grin and shiny black eyes. Jessie was larger, well-rounded, with bright blue eyes.

"Don't worry. They can be trusted," Mrs. Walker assured them. They probably worked for the same clandestine agency that had recruited Mrs. Walker.

Jessie lingered a little longer than was necessary over Sam's offered hand, her head cocked coquettishly. At least Sam had the grace to blush. In her youth, Jessie must have been a true Southern belle.

Mrs. Walker started the sandwiches around the table. Jennifer took one and passed the plate on. "Hand that back to Jennifer," Mrs. Walker ordered Sam. "She needs to eat more than that, especially now."

"I can't eat," Jennifer declared in a stage whisper. "I want to know what you found out."

Mrs. Walker shook her head stubbornly. "I refuse to begin until you have a decent meal in your stomach."

Jennifer glared defiantly but took two more sandwiches, stuffing a whole one into her mouth. Her father used to make her wait to open her packages until after breakfast on Christmas morning. She hadn't liked that, either.

Fortunately, the wait was mercifully short. Everyone gulped their food.

"Okay," Mrs. Walker opened, leaning in, the orchestra beginning another movement. "We've run down most of the visitors to the building Friday night."

Jessie offered a further explanation. "We eliminated children, sisters, brothers, nephews, cousins, etcetera, who come and go, visiting their relatives on a regular basis."

Mae Belle nodded. "It's highly unlikely one of them took time from a routine visit to commit a murder."

"Okay, so what do you have left?" Sam asked.

Mrs. Walker clucked her tongue at him. "We're getting to that."

"We also took out regular visitors, both male and female, to residents who had no association with Ms. Richmond," Mae Belle went on.

"That left the repairmen and the delivery personnel," Mrs. Walker said.

"I called all the repair services and each one checked out," Mae Belle assured them.

"And I've been working on the delivery companies," Jessie said. "Ernie didn't get the company names of everyone who came into the building that night, so it's taking a bit longer. I've gotten through all the telegram services and about half the florists in the area."

"Ernie should know better than that," Mrs. Walker complained. "He's supposed to take the address of every delivery person who walks through that door."

"Of course he is, but I'm afraid he's become a little lax these days," Mae Belle observed.

"We also had one real estate agent and her client looking at one of the units," Jessie said. "The unit is for sale, but I have yet to get the name of the client. We should have more for you in a day or two."

Jennifer hardly knew what to say. Mrs. Walker and her friends were as good as any P.I. agency she could have devised for a novel. "Thank you," she managed. Her words seemed hardly adequate to express her gratitude. "I can't believe you've done all this for me."

"Oh, pish!" Mrs. Walker declared. "Running down a murderer beats a round of bridge any day!" Mae Belle and Jessie nodded enthusiastically.

Mrs. Walker rose to her feet. "I'll get us all some coffee. But remember, dear, all vital communications must be made in person. No exceptions. When I phone you next, it will be to invite you for bridge if we need some additional information, Trivial Pursuit if the police have returned to question me, bingo if we've hit on something important, and Dungeons and Dragons if things have taken a particularly dark turn."

Jennifer had never had any desire to play Dungeons and Dragons, and she certainly hoped she wouldn't be required to now.

"Have you got all that?" Mrs. Walker asked.

"We've got it," Sam assured her.

"Good."

"Mrs. Walker, the last time I saw you, you mentioned that Kyle Browning was seeing Penney Richmond."

"But of course. I nearly forgot. I put Jessie on it right away, not more than an hour after you left."

Jessie's mouth curved into an impish grin.

"You see, Mr. Staunton has had quite a crush on Jessie for some time, nearly a year, since he first moved into the building."

"But she's never given him a tumble. He's *way* too old for her," Mae Belle added.

Jennifer wondered where this story was heading and if she were old enough to hear it. While she was sure Jessie's love life held a certain morbid fascination, she was having trouble relating it to Penney Richmond's murder.

"So I called her up and told her to go for it, and I'm afraid she did just that, sacrificed herself for justice."

Uh-oh. Jennifer definitely did not want to go where this conversation was heading.

"The point being . . ."

"The point is that Mr. Staunton lives only three doors down from Ms. Richmond's apartment. He can confirm that Kyle Browning was a regular visitor to her apartment for a number of months, usually late on a Friday night."

"But get this," Jessie dove in. "He doesn't think they were lovers—no handholding, no flowers, no stolen kisses in the hall, no lingering goodbyes at the door."

"Well, then. If Penney Richmond and Kyle Browning *weren't* lovers, just what were they doing all those Friday nights?" Jennifer asked.

"Indeed. Just what *were* they doing?" Mrs. Walker mused.

Chapter 30

Sam, love his heart, brought Thai peanut noodles in cute, little Chinese takeout boxes for supper. They ate curled up on the sofa, he with chopsticks, she with a fork and knife. He was obviously tired, having worked all afternoon after driving back from Atlanta.

Jennifer felt more relaxed than she had in days. If only this were last Friday night. If only . . . She was playing that stupid head game again. It was time to play that other game her mother had taught her. At least Sam believed she was innocent. At least Mrs. Walker and her O'Hara Tara Irregulars were doing all they could for her. At least her critique group was a hundred percent behind—

"You in there?" Sam asked.

"Unfortunately, yes. I haven't been able to figure out how Monique's heroines slip through those little blips in time to alternate universes."

"Am I supposed to understand what you're talking about?"

"I'd be concerned about you if you did." She stood and reached for Sam's empty carton. "Let me take that."

He caught her hand in midair. "How are you holding up?"

Jennifer shrugged. Should she tell him? Tell him how frightened she really was? How she was worried that Jaimie, who was destined to be another Albert Einstein or Mother Teresa, depending on that pesky gender issue, was most likely never going to be born to discover the true physical and spiritual nature of the universe? Tell him how Maxie Malone's courage never wavered and how she could put together a set of completely unrelated clues and come up with the solution to any perfect crime? And how *she* couldn't solve more than half of those one-minute mysteries her fellow mystery writers were so keen on writing?

"I'm okay," she fudged.

He brought her hand to his lips and kissed it. "That's a lie, but I'll play along if you want me to."

"I want you to." She sank back down to the couch, wishing everything would just go away. He pulled her close to him, her chin resting against his throat.

"Ouch! What the heck—"

"Sorry. Earrings." Jennifer pulled the oversized hoops from her ears, threw them on the coffee table, and settled her cheek back down into the crook of Sam's neck.

This was nice. She could get used to it. She could be content to stay there forever, ignoring the world, ignoring the very real possibility that if Sam were the one she'd been waiting for, she'd waited a little too long.

And there was that nagging voice again, a little person's voice complaining loudly in her heart that if Mommy didn't get off her duff and clear her name, he or she was fated to oblivion.

Jennifer sat up.

"What's the matter?" Sam asked.

"We need to know what Browning was doing those Friday nights at Richmond's apartment."

"What comes naturally?" Sam suggested.

Jennifer shook her head. "You heard what Mr. Staunton told Jessie. He might be old, but he seems to remember sufficiently well what constitutes a romance to know that Penney and Kyle were having none of it. Staunton certainly knew what to do with Jessie. Besides, there is no way a man like Browning could find that Richmond woman attractive." Nor could any other man who wasn't deaf and half blind and not a fan of fairy-tale witches, she added to herself, fully aware she might be just a tad prejudiced against ol' Penney.

"Browning must have had a manuscript," Jennifer continued. "Not the one I showed you that I took from his office, but another, publishable work."

"So he buckled down and wrote it."

"I don't think so. The rejection letter from Richmond's agency was dated only a year ago, and Browning's been dead about four months. He had a lot to learn to put together a decent book in that time. I don't think he could do it. As fast as I write, I've never been able to complete a first draft in less than five, and then there are the revisions. Remember, the man had no concept of the form."

"So you think Richmond was helping him with a manuscript?"

"Possibly. She could have made really big bucks off a successful Browning book. He was nationally known, and that scandal with the hurricane was a journalist's field day. But that still doesn't tell us where the manuscript came from. Richmond could help polish, but I hardly think she would have written it for him. We don't even know if she *could* write."

"You think he used a ghost writer?"

"Most likely."

"Do you have any idea who?"

"All I know for sure is two people were having private meetings and both of them are dead."

A thump sounded on the door, followed by two more.

A shot of adrenaline sped through Jennifer's body.

Muffy's barks echoed from the bathroom, and Jennifer could hear the infernal ringing of the bathtub.

Sam put a finger to his lips and motioned for her to go to the door.

She peered through the peephole, Sam at her shoulder. Edith Warfield's face stared back at her. What the heck was Edith doing at her door?

Sam strained past Jennifer to get a look.

With a great push that sent Sam in the direction of the coffee table, Jennifer frantically motioned toward the empty cartons. Sam scooped up the remains of their dinner and headed to the back of the apartment. She opened the door a crack. "Yes?"

"Jennifer, I need to speak to you."

"What about?"

"Nothing I can talk about in the hallway. Please. Let me come in."

Sam had made it to the bedroom. Jennifer heard the faint click of the latch as she swung wide the door. She gestured toward the sofa, and Edith took up residence where Sam had so recently been sitting. If she sensed any lingering scent from his aftershave, she seemed too preoccupied to notice. She sat there with her coat on, clutching her purse in her lap.

"You seem like a nice girl. I don't know what you've got yourself involved with, but I felt it was my duty to warn you. The police called us in yesterday morning—Steve, John, and myself. They asked all kinds of questions about you, your qualifications, how you got the job. . . . They seem to think that your coming to work at Channel 14 last week might somehow be connected to the death of that poor woman in Atlanta." Edith shuddered.

"And what did you tell them?"

"Not much. Steve said he'd met you at a party you catered, John's wedding, actually, and that he offered you a job doing the food for the party celebrating the sale of his book. Is that true? Were you at that party?"

Jennifer shoved an imaginary tray in the other woman's direction. "Canapé?"

"Oh, Lord, that was you, wasn't it?"

Jennifer nodded. "That's how I make my money."

"It's just that with Steve, one never knows."

Oh, great. Edith probably thought he'd picked her up on Hooker Avenue. And she had just started to like Edith, too.

"I read about your arrest in the paper, and about the fact that you're a mystery writer. I suppose the dead woman was your agent."

A cynical smile settled in the corner of Jennifer's mouth. "No. As a matter of fact, I'd never met her."

"Goodness. And yet the police . . ." Edith pulled a tissue from her purse and ran it over her face.

"What is it I can do for you?" Jennifer asked.

"Could you get me a glass of water?"

That wasn't exactly the answer Jennifer had in mind.

But it seemed like the least she could do for a woman who had come all the way from wherever the heck it was she'd come from to tell her whatever the heck it was she was there to say.

Jennifer slipped into the kitchen and filled a glass with ice and tap water. She brought it back to Edith, who gulped it appreciatively.

"Thanks. It hasn't been that long since Kyle . . ." Edith cleared her throat. "You'll have to excuse me. It seems that tragedy is hitting too close to home these days." Edith stared at her solemnly. "I'm sure you're wondering why I'm here. It's Steve. I'm worried about him."

Worried? About Moore? Did people worry about the Steve Moores of this world?

"Oh, I know you probably think he's a wretched man the way he chases after attractive young women like yourself."

Wretched was one term. Jennifer had others.

"But there's more to the man than . . . his preoccupation with the physical."

Sex. The word was sex. Jennifer didn't mind that Edith was talking in the abstract as long as she wasn't expected to comment using the same genteel language. The man was a lech, plain and simple. She'd been too busy keeping him at arm's length to consider any other aspects of his personality.

"He and Kyle were close. Kyle's suicide hit him hard. Neither had any real family to speak of, no one to care, no one to turn to. It's just that I'm afraid now that Steve's agent is dead and at a time when things seemed to be going so well for him at last . . . You see, he's had several bouts with depression, clinical depression. He's been hospitalized twice. I think maybe that's why he's like he is."

Edith paused to again clear her throat. She seemed actually choked up over Mr. Sleaze.

"What is it you want from me?" Jennifer asked.

"Steve likes you."

Jennifer made a face. She couldn't help it. Honest.

"No, I mean he genuinely likes you, not only in the way you're thinking. He needs a friend right now. I . . . I'm afraid of what he might do to himself. And there is no one."

"How about you?" Jennifer asked. She wasn't about to go into the lion's den alone if she could help it.

Edith shook her head slowly. "He asked me to come here. He wants to see you Friday night at his house, at ten o'clock. We don't want another tragedy. And don't worry, he won't hurt you. I promise you that. You won't have to stay long."

Edith rose to go. "I need your word that you'll be there."

And Jennifer needed a bodyguard.

"Could you live with yourself if you denied him this one meeting? I've known Steve for years. I wouldn't ask you to go if I weren't confident that you'll be safe."

Edith was convincing. Maybe Jennifer could stop by for a few minutes. Tell ol' Steve to hang in there. And get the heck out of there.

"Will you come?" Edith pressed.

Jennifer nodded.

Edith let out the breath she'd been holding. "Thank you. You've been a tremendous help. And as for your problems over this Richmond woman's death, if there's anything I can do . . ."

"Thanks," Jennifer told her, walking her to the door. "I'll remember that."

She'd barely closed the door and locked it when she found Sam standing behind her.

"What was—"

Jennifer shushed him as she watched Edith disappear out of the view of the peephole.

She turned back to Sam, a puzzled look on her face. "I don't know. She wants me to see Steve Moore."

"What for?"

"That's the part I don't understand. She seems to think he may be suicidal."

"That oily . . . He's no more suicidal than Kyle Browning. When does she want you to go?"

"Friday night. Ten o'clock. His house."

"Where we catered his book party."

"Right."

"Okay. I can make that."

"You?"

"You go in; I'll stay in the car. I'll give you, say, fifteen minutes. Any more than that and I'm at the creep's door. Besides, you could learn a lot in fifteen minutes."

About things she'd rather not know. But if Steve Moore was looking toward her as a confidante, she could hardly pass up the opportunity. The police had far too much evidence against her, and she had far too little to steer them in another direction.

Sam took her hand and drew her back to the couch. "Let's see if we can't remember where we were before we were interrupted." He pulled Jennifer to him.

She tried to relax. Really, she did. But an uneasy feeling had broken the mood. What did Steve Moore want with her?

Chapter 31

Teri slammed the door to Jennifer's apartment behind her and collapsed against it, Muffy dancing about her knees. "Don't you *ever* send me off on a covert assignment with that woman again!"

Jennifer stared at Teri, whose dark complexion was flushed. If she recalled correctly, Leigh Ann had volunteered to go to Atlanta to check out Richmond's literary agency and had asked Teri to go with her.

"Where's Leigh Ann?" Jennifer asked suspiciously.

"Parking the car. She'll be up in a minute."

At least she was still alive. But then, of course, Leigh Ann would be. She was small, wily, and remarkably resourceful.

"How'd it go at the agency?" Jennifer asked.

Teri stripped off her jacket and dumped it on a chair, walked out of her shoes, and collapsed on the sofa. Muffy followed her and took up residence at her side, Teri's hand dangling down to absently stroke the dog's ears.

"What's the strongest thing you've got to drink?" Teri asked.

"Wine."

"I'll take it."

Jennifer retrieved the bottle from the refrigerator, filled

a juice glass, and brought it back to Teri just as two dainty raps sounded. Muffy let out a bark and scampered, tail wagging, to the door.

"Don't let her in. You'll be sorry if you do," Teri warned.

Jennifer swung open the door. Leigh Ann looked as if she'd stepped out of a wind tunnel, her brunette bangs board straight and hanging in her grim, green eyes. "Don't you *ever* ask me to go anywhere with that woman again," she choked, pointing an accusing finger in Teri's direction.

Teri flinched. "Me? Me?"

At that moment, Jennifer didn't want to know what happened at Richmond's agency. She wanted to lock the two of them in a closet while she went out, preferably for an ice cream sundae. If one were still alive when she got back, she'd be glad to listen to her version. But then, Jennifer seldom did what she wanted to do.

She pulled Leigh Ann inside and bolted the door. Muffy jumped up and gave Leigh Ann a welcoming hand bath. Dogs. The lucky creatures couldn't understand more than a handful of words, one of which was *good*.

Leigh Ann petted Muffy's head and then brushed her away. She added her jacket to Teri's and took a deep breath. "I—"

"You," Jennifer interrupted, "over there." She pointed to the upholstered chair at the end of the couch. Leigh Ann obediently sat down.

"This woman—" Teri started.

Jennifer pointed her finger. "Not *one* word." She spoke with such strength even she herself would have shut up.

Jennifer brought a straight-back chair from the dining area, drew it up close to the coffee table, and sat down.

"Obviously things did not go well. Calm down and tell me what happened—and leave out the accusations." She nodded toward Teri.

"After our experience at Channel 14 the other day, I thought Leigh Ann and I should have a plan. I mean, you can't just waltz into an office for no reason. So I decided we'd present ourselves as co-authors who had an appointment with Penney Richmond."

"Co-authors, neither of whom read in the paper, heard on the radio, or watched on TV that Richmond had been murdered," Leigh Ann threw in sarcastically.

"I would bet *most* people in Georgia don't know who Penney Richmond was, let alone that she's dead," Teri said.

"True, but did you have to tell the receptionist our National Guard unit had been called up and we were in some made-up island country for the past two weeks? Trapped in a cave-in while spelunking—now that would have been more believable."

"She bought it, didn't she?"

Leigh Ann gave Teri one of those you-idiot looks. "No, she just didn't call us on it. There's a difference. If she'd been a bank teller, she would have been pushing that little red button under the counter as she smiled up at us sweetly."

"Okay, okay," Jennifer intervened. "So you tell the woman you didn't know Penney was dead and that you came to keep your appointment. Then what?"

"Of course, no record of any appointment existed because, as you know, we never had one," Leigh Ann said.

"So then I asked to see one of Richmond's associates," Teri explained.

"Only she doesn't have any," Leigh Ann said. "Apparently she ran the last one off over a year ago."

"And then Leigh Ann starts demanding that the agency return our manuscript."

"The one that doesn't exist," Jennifer stated.

"Right," Teri agreed. "She's throwing a real fit—actually, that was quite well done." Teri threw a begrudging look of admiration in Leigh Ann's direction. "She was so demanding, the poor woman never questioned the manuscript's existence. She just pulled up the computer log-in file and started frantically scanning through it, looking for a book by Austin and Brontë."

"You didn't," Jennifer sighed in disbelief.

"I was thinking on my feet," Teri insisted. "The woman didn't blink an eye, did she, Leigh Ann?"

"Not once," Leigh Ann agreed. "We told her we'd submitted it almost a year ago, but we didn't get our self-addressed, stamped postcard back until four months ago."

"Clever. So she was searching the period when Kyle Browning might have submitted something."

"Right," Teri said.

"Sounds great," Jennifer said.

Leigh Ann nodded. "Everything was going relatively well up until the fire."

"The fire?" Jennifer asked, almost sorry she'd let the words escape her mouth.

"Teri gives me some screwy hand signal behind the receptionist's back—"

"It was the American Sign Language symbol for *print*. Thumb and second finger of the right hand drawn together and placed on the open palm of the left hand."

"I've never had a deaf character, like some people I

know. You might have checked with me to see if I *knew* sign language."

"Wasn't time. Besides, all those symbols are based on common sense."

"Let's talk about common—"

"No, let's not," Jennifer interrupted. "Teri gives you this indecipherable sign—"

"Don't take sides, Jennifer," Teri cautioned.

Jennifer acknowledged Teri's point with a nod. Mediating this conversation was a suicide mission at best. "Teri gives you this sign and then what?"

"She clutches her stomach, says she's going to be sick, and runs out of the room, leaving me with this poor woman madly looking through screens of entries for something that isn't there. A few seconds later the fire alarm goes off."

"Teri had gone into the hall and pulled the alarm?" Jennifer asked.

"You'd think so, wouldn't you?" Leigh Ann growled. "She'd gone in the bathroom and started a fire in the trash can. It didn't *occur* to her just to pull the alarm."

Teri was right. She didn't improvise well.

"People started running up and down the halls, and the receptionist lost it," Leigh Ann said. "I mean the woman was in a state of panic. I found her purse and sent her out the door. I told her not to worry. I'd turn off the computer and follow her out. Of course, instead I printed out the entries, about twenty pages in all, single-spaced."

"Just like I signaled for you to do."

Leigh Ann glared at Teri. "And then the sprinkler system went off."

"Where were you while all this was going on?" Jennifer asked Teri.

"I was getting a little concerned about the fire. Man, those paper towels really go up! So I went back to the bathroom, but like Leigh Ann said, the sprinkler system went off and it drenched me and the trash can—"

Leigh Ann blew her ruined bangs away from her forehead. "Not to mention me and Richmond's office and the sheets coming out of the printer.

"Here," Leigh Ann offered, pulling a crumpled mess of paper from her pants' pocket. "For what it's worth. Here's a list of all the complete manuscripts logged in at Richmond's agency during that eight-month period."

Jennifer took the water-stained sheets from Leigh Ann's hand. "Thanks. You guys are pros. Maxie Malone couldn't have done better herself."

"Now, that's a compliment, wouldn't you say, partner?" Teri threw Leigh Ann a sheepish look.

"I didn't really mean it when I said you were lucky you didn't drown like a turkey in the rain in the rest room," Leigh Ann confessed.

"And I'm sorry about that crack I made about you throwing yourself in front of that fireman on the way out of the building."

"I slipped, really I did, just like I told you."

"I know you did, even if he was the most gorgeous hunk of a man I've seen in a long time. I saw your foot hit that puddle of water in the lobby."

If there was anything more irritating than hearing two friends fight, it was listening to them trying to make up. Fortunately, the phone rang.

"Hello," Jennifer sang into the receiver, grateful someone, anyone, had taken her away from Teri and Leigh Ann.

Mrs. Walker's voice came over the wire. "I thought you and that nice friend of yours might enjoy a little game, say tomorrow morning, about eleven? We'll meet you at that quaint little café where we first met."

"Game?" Jennifer asked, her mouth going dry. "What kind of game?"

"Bingo, dear. Bingo."

Chapter 32

"Why are you wearing only one earring?" Sam asked, taking a sip of hazelnut coffee, Friday's special of the day at Atlanta's Café on the Corner.

Jennifer fingered her right earlobe, the one with the large gold hoop. "I can't find the other one. I thought maybe I'd left it in your car, so I put this one on to remind me to look for it."

"Is *that* why you were rooting around on the floorboard on the way over here?"

"Pigs root. I was looking." She took another sip of her chocolate raspberry coffee and checked her watch. Two minutes before eleven. She looked up to see Mrs. Walker, Jessie, and Mae Belle in tow, heading straight toward them.

Jessie's face was a deep pink. "You wouldn't think, I mean, it's why children have nightmares, for Heaven's sake," she sputtered.

"Stop babbling and pull up something to sit on," Mrs. Walker ordered, squeezing three more chairs around the tiny round table.

A waitress in an earth-brown caftan approached, but Mrs. Walker shooed her away. "We'll order later, Lori. I'll let you know when."

The woman backed up with an uncertain look on her face.

Mrs. Walker waited until Lori was safely behind the counter and then leaned in like a coach in a huddle at a football game. "Here's the deal. We can't account for the clown."

The clown. A cold chill swept through Jennifer. She'd walked right past a clown on Penney Richmond's floor the night of the murder, a clown with evil eyes.

"Ernie said he was there to deliver a big bunch of helium balloons, and he didn't have any when he left," Jessie gasped out. "But none of the florists or balloon shops have any record of a delivery to O'Hara's Tara scheduled for that night."

"What did this clown look and sound like?" Sam asked.

"No no no," Mae Belle said. "You're missing the point. Ernie says he couldn't recognize him under any circumstances. He was in full makeup with baggy clothes, big shoes . . . and he wouldn't talk, only mime, playing two parts, the giver and the receiver. He made a big elaborate bow as though offering the bouquet to someone, and then had Ernie hold it as he pretended to be so surprised and delighted to be receiving it. Several people applauded. Ernie waved him on up."

"Don't forget the gloves," Jessie chimed in. "He had on white, cotton gloves." She nodded knowingly.

"But no one seems to have gotten the balloons," Mrs. Walker pointed out.

"Could the police have found them in that Richmond woman's apartment," Mae Belle asked, "and not mentioned it? I understand they often don't put details in the newspaper so they can tell if someone really has inside information about a crime. Keeps the loonies from making fake confessions."

"All he had to do was step out on the balcony," Jennifer said, "and simply let them go. With no trees to get caught in, who knows where they wound up."

"Well that's it, then," Mrs. Walker declared. "The police need to find this clown and arrest him for murder."

If only it were that simple. Jennifer could just hear the APB now: "Be on the lookout for white-faced suspect with large red nose, big orange mouth, curly, rainbow-colored hair, and threatening eyes that look like they belong to the devil himself."

And why would they bother chasing some clown when they already had a bird in the hand—her? The choice was ridiculously obvious. Pursue evidence against a woman in a wig sporting a false pregnancy who had written threatening letters to the victim in her own handwriting or chase after some clown making a balloon delivery? She knew which one she'd suspect, and she knew which one the police would prosecute for murder.

It was close to eight o'clock. Jennifer was exhausted, and she still had to meet with Steve Moore that night. Sam would be back at her house at nine-thirty. She'd really like to take a nap, but sleep would not come easily, especially after the drive back from Atlanta. Sam was worried, although he tried not to show it. He hardly spoke to her the whole way back. He had kissed her good night, but it felt more like a last kiss to a condemned prisoner than the promise of a budding romance. Bars really put a dent in one's love life.

Jennifer took a sip of the hot tea she'd just made and

crossed her legs on the coffee table. Muffy snuggled close and rested her head on Jennifer's knees. She was a needy little creature. What would happen to Muffy if she were sent to the Big House? Dee Dee or Sam would have to take her. Dee Dee already had a cat, and Muffy hated going there even for a day. But Sam's schedule was so erratic . . .

She stroked Muffy's head as she took up the water-streaked sheets Leigh Ann had given her. She'd scanned all twenty pages the night before for Browning's name, a name she'd never found. She'd sat down only minutes ago to look for Steve Moore's name and manuscript. Again, she didn't find it on the list.

She paused. Since Penney knew both Browning and Moore personally, they could have handed their manuscripts to her rather than mailing them. Is that why neither appeared on the list? Jennifer shook her head. From everything she had seen, Richmond was nothing if not efficient—diabolical and hard-hearted, but still efficient. They should be there.

Maybe she'd missed the entry. Maybe it was coded in some way and that was why she couldn't find it by scanning. She'd have to examine each line, carefully, both name and title.

She took another gulp of tea. Twenty pages, single-spaced. This would take some time.

It did. By page six she felt like she was seeing double. She rubbed her eyes. How was she going to get out of the mess she was in? Maybe she wasn't. She was sure now that the clown was the murderer. Here she was, an eye-witness. She'd actually seen the killer, and a fat lot of good that did. She didn't even know if Clarabelle was male or female. Actually, it was a great idea for a disguise. She could use it in a novel sometime, only no one would believe it—too corny.

She yawned and took up page seven. A third of the way down was a submission by E. Warfield. Jennifer stopped and blinked. The title of the book was listed as *Scandal to Truth: The Story the Media Didn't Tell*.

Jennifer couldn't take her eyes from the page. In one overwhelming moment of understanding, everything fell into place. *She knew.* She knew just like Sherlock Holmes, Miss Marple, Peter Wimsey, Maxie Malone, and even Jolene Arizona would know. She knew who killed Kyle Browning, who killed Penney Richmond—and why. And who, if she didn't do something quick, was about to kill again.

Chapter 33

Jennifer grabbed the phone and punched in Sam's number. His cheery voice came from his answering machine. Didn't he know she needed to talk to him? *Now.* Not later. And, no, she didn't care that her call was important to him or that he would return it as soon as possible, and she most certainly didn't intend to have a good day!

Impatiently she waited for the beep. "Why aren't you home?" she sputtered. "I need you this minute. If I'm right, Steve Moore will be victim number three. I'm going to try to get in touch with him, to warn him. I don't dare wait until nine-thirty for you to get here."

She slammed down the receiver and reached for the phone book. Moore's number was unlisted—of course—and she'd thrown out his card.

She dialed Dee Dee. Her husband picked up the phone. "Sorry, Jen, she's off on a job with April, but I couldn't tell you where."

"What about her Rolodex?"

"She takes it with her. You know that."

She did know that. She also knew that in the current situation Dee Dee's husband John was totally useless. She bid him farewell in mid-sentence.

She had no options. She had no allies. She certainly couldn't drag Teri or Leigh Ann with her, even if she could find them on a Friday night. That'd be like taking along the Keystone Kops. She'd have to go it alone, like Maxie Malone would. But Maxie was so much better at all this than she could ever hope to be. Maxie was courageous. Maxie knew how to handle herself. Maxie was fictional.

Jennifer threw on a light jacket and picked up her shoulder bag. Muffy whined and pattered after her toward the door. Jennifer turned, cupped the dog's face in her hands, and rubbed her briskly behind her ears. "I love you, baby," she said as though saying goodbye to a dear friend for the last time.

Jennifer had always avoided dealing with real life in an up-close, personal way. Whatever happened tonight, she'd made the plunge. She just hoped it wasn't straight off a cliff.

The outside of Moore's house was dark except for the porch light. He was, after all, expecting her later. Jennifer pulled into the drive behind a utilitarian blue Chevrolet— not exactly the babe magnet she'd expected Moore to drive—and cut the engine. At least he was home and she hadn't driven all the way out here for nothing.

No lights from neighboring houses were visible, and the early evening dark was beginning to clothe the area in its shroud. The houses were set so far apart, it gave each lot a feeling of isolation.

Jennifer took a deep breath. What was she going to say to Moore? Would he laugh in her face when she said she believed his life was in danger? It didn't really matter what he did. She had to do what she had to do.

She slipped out of the car and made her way up to the front door. Her hand was poised to knock when she heard something, a laugh, a deep baritone chuckle echo down the hall. She leaned forward and pressed her ear to the wood.

Jennifer could detect no sound from a TV or radio. No music. Then she heard the faint tones of a woman's voice. It sounded as if Moore had one of his women friends in. And he was expecting her at ten. What was the creep doing? Running them in shifts?

She couldn't very well ring the bell, excuse herself for interrupting, and say, "Oh, by the way, I just dropped by to warn you that someone is going to murder you. Have a good evening."

No. She'd have to assess the situation.

If Moore and the woman were in the den, she'd be able to get a peek through the French doors around back. If they were in the bedroom . . . She shuddered. They'd better be in the den.

She followed the outside of the house around to the back, cursing herself for not bringing a flashlight. A soft glow spilled from the French doors onto the brick patio. Thank goodness Steve Moore lived in the house alone. A woman would have had curtains over those windows two minutes after crossing the threshold. She snuck up to the brick wall, held her breath, and leaned forward to peer in.

Moore was standing next to the sofa, a smile on his face, a wineglass in one hand. He was listening to a woman sitting directly in front of him on an ottoman. Her hair was soft on her shoulders, teasing the silky fabric of her dress. Her long, full skirt broke at the knee and brushed the middle of her calf. Her stockinged feet were crossed and stretched coquettishly to one side. She threw back her head and laughed, and then raised a bottle of wine toward Moore, bringing her face into profile.

Edith. Oh, God! It was Edith.

A terrible thought flashed through her mind. What if Edith had brought poisoned wine just like her murderer in *The Last Goodbye Toast*?

Jennifer had to do something quickly. She stepped right in front of the window and frantically waved her arms over her head like a crewman bringing a plane in for landing.

Moore didn't even blink in her direction. Edith poured wine into Moore's glass and then filled her own. They clinked glasses, and she splashed some into her lap. She got up, rubbing at her skirt, and left the room. It had to be poison.

A stupid smile played on Moore's lips as he brought his glass dangerously close to his lips.

Jennifer pounded on the door with her fist, and Moore turned, a puzzled look on his face.

She fanned her hands back and forth in what she hoped was the universal sign for *no* and then cupped a pretend glass as though drinking from it.

Moore frowned and came toward the door. "What are you doing here? Can't you see I'm busy?" he asked through the glass.

"Don't *drink* the *wine*," Jennifer called out in a whisper she prayed he could hear.

"What?" Moore asked.

"The wine!" Jennifer shouted, abandoning all pretense of discretion. "Don't drink it. It's poison."

"I can't hear you through this glass," Moore insisted. "It sounds like you're saying something about poison."

He opened the door, and Jennifer grabbed the wine from his hand and poured it on the ground.

"Have you lost your mind?"

"It was Edith. Edith killed Browning, Edith killed Richmond, and she's about to kill you."

"You must be crazy. What are you doing here?"

"Warning you. Besides, you invited me. I know I'm a little early, but—"

"I most certainly did not. And it's my understanding *you* are the one who killed Penney Richmond. When the police told me you'd gone over the edge, it was hard for me to believe, but now that I see you like—"

"Why don't you ask Miss Marsh in, Steve?" Edith was standing in the doorway, a gun held firmly with both hands and pointed in their direction.

"See. I told you," Jennifer whispered.

"Come on in, Jennifer. You're a little early, but this will do just as well. I'd planned on your standing trial for the murders, but I guess the state won't mind if we save them a bit of money."

Moore was standing almost directly in front of her. For a brief moment she considered giving him a push, propelling him in Edith's direction. She might actually be able to escape into the outside darkness. But then again, she might not. In either case, Moore was sure to wind up dead. Edith couldn't chase her and hold a gun on Moore at the same time. And after all, she had come there to save him, not precipitate his death.

Jennifer sighed and obediently followed Moore into the room. Edith motioned them toward the sofa with a wave of the gun barrel.

"Sit," Edith ordered. "I did tell you *ten* o'clock, didn't I?"

Jennifer nodded, sinking onto the couch. "Why did you ask me to come?"

Edith shrugged. "It's not that I dislike you, Jennifer. In many ways, you remind me of my younger self. But the police are quite ready to believe you killed Penney Richmond. I thought if they believed that, they could as easily believe you killed an unimaginative lover-boy like Steve here."

"Unimaginative?" Moore grumbled.

"And you planned somehow to frame *me* for it?"

Edith shifted the gun to one hand and pulled a large, gold, hoop earring from her skirt pocket, dangling it on one finger.

Jennifer stared in disbelief. "I've been looking all over—"

Edith stuffed it back into her pocket. "You shouldn't leave your jewelry lying around where anyone can pick it up."

Whatever sympathy Jennifer felt for Edith was rapidly disappearing. The woman was a jewelry-swiping, writer-framing psychopath.

Steve opened his mouth, but Edith cut him off. "Save it, you thieving—"

Jennifer put up her hand as if asking a question in school. "Ah, excuse me. I don't think he knows."

"Knows what?" Moore looked thoroughly confused.

"Browning's manuscript," Jennifer said. "He didn't write it, at least not in the conventional sense."

A look of surprise spread over Edith's features. "Aren't you the clever little detective."

"What do you mean he didn't write it?" By this time Moore was red in the face, and Jennifer wondered if he were on medication for high blood pressure. An aneurism about now would defeat her reason for being there.

"Richmond wanted a manuscript from Browning, but he couldn't get it together." Jennifer looked to Edith for agreement.

"Go on," Edith ordered.

"Very well. Browning was a good TV journalist, but he had no concept of how to structure a book. Richmond was urging him to get with it and produce a salable manuscript. She was, after all, the most high-powered agent, as well as the most unethical, in the area. Edith had a manuscript—apparently a good one."

Edith nodded. "Damn good."

"She sent it to Richmond, who must have copied it. I'm guessing she used it for the basis of Browning's book, used the structure, the opening events, following the basic outline, including all the pertinent details. How close am I?"

"Close enough. Richmond had the audacity to toss my book back at me saying it was unmarketable. I didn't have a name to carry a scandal book."

"Maybe she was right," Moore offered.

Edith's grip tightened on the gun. "Don't give me that. Every maid and babysitter write exposés."

Jennifer stared at Moore thoughtfully. "Moore's too stupid to live. I think you're right. He deserves to be shot."

"I was there—at Browning's side. I heard and saw it all firsthand," Edith spat out. "And I was the only one willing to tell it like it was."

"The only one both willing and able to write it," Jennifer added.

"And then when Kyle died, *you* took up the project . . ." Edith shook the gun in Moore's direction. "As if you had any right."

"My dear Edith . . ." Moore began.

Jennifer rolled her eyes. Charm, especially Moore's version of what passed for charm, was not going to have much sway over Edith.

". . . Penney thought the book would be more successful with someone to promote it on tour," Moore continued. "She thought we could finish the manuscript, use Kyle's death as a springboard and me as his spokesperson. If I'd had any idea—"

"How did you find out?" Jennifer asked Edith, hoping to distract her.

"That idiot Browning had me work on the manuscript. He and that woman would meet on Friday nights, and he would come in with handwritten pages every Monday morning. It became increasingly obvious I had typed the same manuscript before."

"He must not have known," Jennifer said. "No one could be that—"

"He knew when I told him—that afternoon on the roof."

"You told him and he jumped off?" Moore seemed astounded.

Jennifer and Edith exchanged looks. "Maybe we could take turns shooting him," Jennifer suggested.

"What did happen on that roof?" Jennifer asked. "Browning must have been standing by the wall and—"

"I got angry. He suggested I might work as a ghost writer on the manuscript. Can you believe it? My own manuscript."

"And you pushed him," Jennifer said.

"Pushed, shoved, whatever. Actually it was more like pounding my fists into his chest. I didn't mean for him to go over, but the wall caught him at an awkward spot, and before I realized what was happening, he was gone."

"And then—with Kyle hardly cold in his grave—Moore, here, took up the work. At Richmond's request," Jennifer concluded.

"At Richmond's request," Edith repeated. Her face took on an ugly purplish hue at the mention of Richmond's name. She took two deep breaths and then turned curiously toward Jennifer.

"How'd you know? How'd you know I killed them?" she asked.

"I saw you," Jennifer said. Well, it was the truth, and bringing up Teri, Leigh Ann, and the fire didn't seem like a smart thing to do, everything considered.

"What?" Edith suddenly seemed off balance.

Jennifer rushed to take advantage. "I saw you—that night at O'Hara's Tara—in the elevator and then on Penney Richmond's floor."

"You couldn't have . . ."

"White face, red nose, rainbow hair, balloons, and not the most attractive ensemble."

"What the—" Moore started, but Jennifer threw him a warning look.

Edith seemed truly shaken. For just a second she lowered the gun and then raised it again. She shook her head.

"Do you remember passing a pregnant woman—long curly black hair, mud-colored sweater, frumpy dress?"

"Pregnant? I thought she was just fat. Oh, my . . ." Edith's jaw dropped. "Don't tell me that was . . ."

"Absolutely. And those threatening letters to Penney Richmond they mentioned in the newspaper, I meant every word. The woman was a fiend. I was there that night to kill her." Not really, but she had to develop some camaraderie with Edith beyond their mutual disdain for Moore.

"But I passed you coming away from her apartment. She was still alive. . . ."

"It was the gun," Jennifer said, as though that said it all.

"It jammed?" Moore threw in.

Both Jennifer and Edith turned toward him with a who-invited-you-into-this-conversation stare. He shut up, apparently smart enough, at last, to realize bringing attention to himself was not such a good idea.

"It belonged to my father," Jennifer explained.

Edith nodded knowingly.

"But why did you want to kill her?" Edith asked.

Good question. The fact that she never intended to kill Richmond and was only doing research for a book wouldn't cut it. She'd have to come up with something Edith could relate to.

Of course—vengeance.

"I write science fiction novels—in addition to mysteries," she lied. "I even had one published."

"Title?"

"Moons of Death."

"I've never heard of it."

"Of course you haven't. Penney was my agent. She was in the business for the money and only the money. Not to promote a writer's career, like most agents. She wanted her cash as fast and as easy as she could get it."

She obviously wasn't telling Edith anything she didn't already know, which was exactly the way she wanted it. "Sales for the book weren't high. When I submitted a synopsis for a second book, she stole the universe I had created and most of the plot." Silently she thanked Monique.

"You know, Jennifer, I really hate to have to kill you."

"Then don't. I mean, Moore's got to go. We're both in agreement on that. Right?"

Edith nodded.

Moore cringed, his eyes darting fervently about the room. Jennifer prayed he wouldn't try anything, no sudden movements. He could easily ruin her plan.

"We can frame Moore for Richmond's murder and dispose of his body—make it look like he panicked and ran off. We'll plant the clown suit and the murder weapon in his bedroom. The police still think Browning jumped off that roof on his own. And even if they don't, they'll never have enough evidence to prove otherwise."

Edith stared at her.

"Believe me, Edith, we can do it. The police will never find him. I've disposed of bodies before."

Chapter 34

"Disposed of bodies?" Moore squeaked out.

"Not real bodies," Jennifer confessed, easing up from the couch and moving to stand in front of the fireplace so Edith could only cover Moore with the gun. "In my books. I did a lot of research. Concrete's the best. Give me a good ol' construction site any day. Piece of cake."

"Where?" Edith asked.

"A new car dealership is going up on the northern end of River Road. Yesterday I noticed a frame for pouring concrete had been put up."

"Isn't that a little shallow?"

Jennifer shook her head. "Those blocks are a good two to three feet thick, especially in the area where they do the repairs and have all that hydraulic equipment. You don't see the thickness of the foundation because it's dug out. My dad ran a construction company. I know about these things." Actually, she knew nothing about them. Her father had been a teacher, and she had no idea how deep a concrete pad needed to be to hold anything. She was banking that Edith was just as ignorant as she was.

"What would we have to do?" Edith asked, not blinking an eye. Inwardly, Jennifer sighed her relief.

"We'll wrap the body in plastic. You got any plastic around here?" Jennifer asked Moore.

If Moore had been apoplectic before, he was now close to a stroke. She thought it better not to include him further in this conversation.

Jennifer shrugged. "Well, no matter. We'll find something that will do. We'll need a couple of shovels to dig out the gravel. And it would help if we had something to carry the excess dirt away when we get done, so it doesn't look like the work site has been disturbed. This house is on a big lot. I bet it requires a lot of yard work. Moore's got to have most of what we need in his outbuilding. He probably has the plastic out there, too, the kind used to keep down weeds. If not, we can use blankets."

"When do we kill him?" Edith asked, nodding in Moore's direction. He was making a whimpering sound.

"Later. Not here. We want the police to believe he's still alive, which means no bloodstains in the house. Once we get rid of the body, we'll come back and plant the clown costume and the gun. You still have the costume, don't you?"

"It's at home, but you've got the gun, the one that killed Penney Richmond."

Jennifer stopped cold. "I do?"

"It's in your sofa. I slipped it down between the cushions when I was at your house." Edith looked at her sheepishly. "At the time, it seemed like the thing to do."

"And that?" Jennifer asked, pointing at the gun trained on Moore.

"Don't worry. It's not traceable."

Jennifer didn't want to know what kind of crime

connections Edith had or what kind of arsenal she'd
built. She let the subject drop.

"We'll need some rope to tie up Moore," Jennifer
pointed out. "I noticed a flashlight in the kitchen drawer
and a collection of keys when I was catering the book
party. You stay here and keep Moore covered while I get
them."

Without a backward look, Jennifer walked out of the
den and into the kitchen. She collapsed for a moment
against the counter, breathing hard. Edith must be buying
her story. She didn't follow her or order her back. Now if
she could just get through this without getting Moore
killed before she got the drop on Edith . . .

She stared at the phone that hung on the wall. Did she
dare dial 911? Some extension phones gave that little
"ding" sound when another phone on the same line was
being dialed, and there was a phone in the den. She
couldn't risk it.

She could arm herself with a knife, but she *hated*
knives. They were so sharp. And where would she hide
one? No, the knives were better left where they were.

She opened the pantry and gave it a quick look-see.
Too bad Moore didn't have an Uzi or at least a shotgun
lurking among the spices. The man was not one to plan
ahead.

Her eyes lit on a spray can of cooking oil. She
snatched it up and placed it on the countertop. Then she
rummaged through the tool drawer, finding the flashlight
and a key ring that was labeled TOOLSHED. Next, she
went to the door to the outside and unlocked it.

When Jennifer got back to the den, Edith had pushed
the ottoman away from the sofa and was now sitting on it

as she made little circles with the gun barrel in Moore's direction. She *really* wanted to pull the trigger.

Edith looked at Jennifer dangling the key ring from her second finger and holding the flashlight with her right. "Found them. Be back in a sec." Jennifer crossed the room and was out the door before Edith had time to react.

Darkness. It'd be so easy, now, to get away. She could get in her car and speed to the nearest police station, or at least a public phone. But what would she tell the police? Moore would testify that she planned to kill him, assuming he were still alive when the police got there. Not only that, but he would testify that if she wasn't actually Penney Richmond's murderer, she was at the very least an accessory. He'd heard her admit to being in Richmond's apartment building that night to kill her.

No, if she were to save Moore, and herself in the process, she needed something other than the police. She needed a colossal distraction.

She doubled back to the kitchen and noiselessly let herself in. She grabbed the can of cooking spray and shook it vigorously. Then she thoroughly coated the tile from the hallway well into the kitchen. That should do it.

Next, she carefully extracted a half-dozen stainless steel forks from the drawer. She laid them in the microwave and set the timer for a full five minutes on High.

Then she stopped up the drain, took down a pot, and turned it upside down in the sink. She plugged in the toaster, placed it atop the saucepan, spread a dish-cloth beneath the faucet, turned on the water, and pressed the lever on the toaster.

She looked once again about the room, shoved the

flashlight deep into her pocket, and silently opened the back door. She took one last, deep breath for courage and pressed her icy index finger against the Start button of the microwave.

A crackling sound accompanied the shower of sparks that began to war inside the appliance. Jennifer dove through the door, rolling onto the grass outside. Recovering her balance, she ran several yards away from the house. And waited. And waited. Maybe all those cautions about metal and microwaves, not to mention toasters and water, were just—

The explosion boomed across the yard, shattering the window above the sink. In almost the same instant, the house went totally dark, silhouetted in the silvery light of the quarter moon.

Wow! She hadn't expected the lights in the den to be on the same circuit as the kitchen. But for all she knew, the circuit box could now be one piece of molten metal. She hoped she hadn't done too much damage. It'd be just her luck to have Moore sue her.

And she hoped there wouldn't be a fire. Fires were not good.

She dashed back toward the house. Silently, she opened the French door to the den and slipped in. She heard a low moan coming from the direction where the couch should be. At least Moore was still alive—sniveling, cowering, but alive.

Echoing down the hallway were a series of oaths. Good. Edith had found the cooking spray.

Jennifer turned on the flashlight and shielded its glare as she made her way to Moore and the couch. He looked alarmingly white in the yellow glow of the beam.

"Jennifer?" he asked.

She placed her fingertips over his lips to shush him.

"Come on," she whispered, dragging his reluctant body up off the couch. "We've got to move fast."

She pulled his arm around her shoulder. His free arm found her waist and squeezed, going for one last grope before he met his Maker. "Let's get the heck out of here," she told him, pushing his arm away.

On the patio, they paused.

"Get!" Jennifer ordered.

Moore stood there, staring.

"Get to the closest neighbor and call the police."

"You mean you're not going to kill me?" Moore choked out.

"Of course not. If you haven't noticed, I'm saving your life. Now go. Call the police before I get myself killed."

Moore turned and fled into the darkness. She only hoped he had some idea where he was going.

Jennifer switched off the flashlight and slipped back into the house. Somewhere in the darkness was a real murderer, a real murderer with a real gun.

"Edith?" Jennifer called out. "Edith, what happened? Are you all right?"

It was, after all, quite possible that Edith hadn't put two and two together, that Edith had no idea that she was responsible for the explosion in the kitchen, and no idea that she was betraying her big-time.

"Jennifer, is that you?" Edith called back. "Where's Moore?"

"I don't know," Jennifer lied. "I can't find him."

"Then get in here and help me up," Edith ordered.

"Every time I try to stand, I slip back down. I think my ankle may be broken."

Jennifer found her way into the hall and headed toward the kitchen, the beam of the flashlight falling across Edith's sprawled body.

A bullet flew past Jennifer's head, tearing through a nearby wall. The flashlight fell from her hand and she dropped to all fours, her palms skating out from under her over the slick, oil-coated tile. She found herself sliding into Edith's body, her chin smack up against the floor.

"You idiot!" Edith spat out in the darkness. "What kind of mystery writer are you that you'd actually think I wouldn't realize *you* were the one behind whatever blew up? No wonder you've never gotten anything published."

Even in the dark, Jennifer saw red. How dare Edith judge her literary skills on her inept personal behavior? Had the woman ever read a word Jennifer had written? No. *Would* she ever read a word Jennifer had written? No. She wouldn't live long enough.

Jennifer dove for what she estimated was Edith's throat. Her elbow connected with an arm, and she rolled over on it, pinning the woman's hand and a most uncomfortable gun beneath her. At the same time, she found Edith's nose and pulled for all she was worth. Under her shoulder blades, she felt the gun loosen as Edith fought to push her off. Jennifer rose up and shoved hard, sending Edith scooting across the slick floor and separating her from the gun. At the same time, Jennifer slid backward, fumbled for the gun, and flung it down the black pit of the hallway.

A rage of adrenaline swept through Jennifer, just as it always did when Jolene Arizona found herself in a fight.

Say what one would about Jolene, she liked to get physical, and the part of Jennifer—granted it was a dark and hidden part—that had given birth to her character was now fully in charge.

"Anyone who hasn't read my work is not allowed to make any comments whatsoever!" Jennifer dove after Edith, who, from the sound of skin slapping against the tile, had yet to find a foothold and was still trapped in a dark, slick world. Flesh connected with flesh, and Jennifer's hand closed on an arm. Sputtering sounds indicated the location of Edith's head. Jennifer turned sideways and threw her body straight out, facedown, on top of where she figured Edith's shoulders had to be, pinning her fast. It was a trick Jolene, an accomplished wrestler, once used to subdue her villain. Of course, Jennifer had no idea, until now, whether it really worked. Edith's body shuddered in a futile attempt to dislodge the weight cradled at her neck and then lay still.

"Get off of me," Edith half screamed, half growled. "You're cutting off my windpipe."

"If that were true, you couldn't talk," Jennifer pointed out. "I'm not moving and neither are you!" she declared. She'd stay there all night if she had to, until Moore found his way to the authorities or until something or someone—

"Jennifer?" a male voice called from the darkness of the den. "Jennifer, are you in there?"

Sam. Thank God. Sam had finally made it. Tears wet her cheeks.

"I'm in the kitchen!" she called back.

A beam of light appeared in the hall and trailed across to the T formed by the two women. "What the—"

"I can't explain now. Don't get too close or you'll find yourself down here with us. There's a gun somewhere in the hall toward the front door. Get it, find the fuse box, see if you can get the lights back on, and please, please, call the police."

Chapter 35

"What's he saying?" Jennifer asked, hovering over Sam as he uh-huhed into the phone. New York publishers didn't call just anyone any day. Thank goodness she'd stopped by the paper to catch a quick lunch with Sam when the call came through.

"I see," he was saying. "No, I'll take care of it. That's right. And thank you for calling." He hung up the phone.

"What'd he say?" Jennifer demanded again, grabbing Sam by the tie and pulling his face within inches of her own.

Carefully, Sam peeled her fingers away from the silky fabric. "He said he was interested." Sam stood up and began shuffling papers on his desk.

Jennifer could hardly contain her joy. The proposal for *The Channel 14 Murders* had been mailed a mere three weeks ago and already had a response.

"He *is* going to buy it, isn't he? I mean, he wouldn't be calling if he weren't serious," she persisted.

Sam turned and faced her. Something was wrong. She could tell. He should be smiling, ecstatic, bubbling like she was. Okay. So she had enough enthusiasm for the both of them, but Sam's steely calm could not be good.

"He had some conditions."

Conditions? She expected changes, revisions, whatever. They were all part of the process.

"He wants the book to come out under my name."

"And mine," she added, and immediately wished she hadn't.

Sam shook his head. "He wants a more . . . objective telling of the story. He says we should downplay your role in all this. Actually, he said you come off . . . too pixilated."

"Pixilated? Ambitious, determined, overfocused maybe, but pixilated?"

"His term, not mine."

Jennifer sank back against the desk.

He cupped her chin. "Look, it's not really all that bad. The book belongs to both of us. We'll split the advance and the profits, if there are any. Besides, what do you care? You want to make your name in fiction."

It was true. And publishing a nonfiction book wouldn't help her all that much in the fiction market. But for one brief moment she had seen her name—Jennifer Marsh—splashed across a book jacket.

"I guess you're right." She sighed.

He kissed her cheek, a sweet, discreet peck, and scooped up a folder from his desk. "I've got to get this copy to my editor before I can take off. I'll be right back."

Jennifer settled into his swivel chair. Disappointment was nothing new to her, but why didn't it ever stop hurting? She'd be impossible to live with for the next two days, if her normal pattern held true, and she intended for Sam to be by her side throughout all the waking moments of those forty-eight hours. It was the least he could do. *His* name would be on the cover.

She picked up a copy of the morning paper and glanced over the front page. Typical newsy day. An article in the lower left-hand corner of the second page caught her eye. It was about a woman in Phoenix who claimed to have dreamed an entire four-hundred-page novel over the course of a week, writing down chapters each day when she awoke. It was being acclaimed as a surreal journey into the subconscious. Following the initial skepticism, two renowned psychologists had flown in to interview her and monitor her sleep process.

Dreams. Murder. Sleepwalking. It'd been done a few years ago, but what if she had a psychic detective who visited crime scenes through out-of-body experiences, and what if he had a spirit guide who—

"Okay, I'm all yours," Sam announced, grabbing his jacket.

Jennifer practically leaped from the chair. "Let's make it dinner or maybe lunch tomorrow. I gotta go before I lose this thought. This one," she beamed, "*this* one's gonna sell!"

A CONVERSATION
WITH JUDY FITZWATER

Q. Judy, Dying to Get Published *is your debut as a novelist. How long did it take to complete? And apart from the cover copy and promotional hoopla, how would you yourself characterize the novel?*

A. It took me about eighteen months to write *Dying to Get Published.* I don't outline, so sometimes I have to wait for inspiration. I was also trying to market an earlier novel, so there were times when I'd receive rejections that would stop me cold and leave me wondering, as does Jennifer, why I was in a business that has so little possibility for success.

Dying to Get Published was great fun to write. It is the story of mystery writer Jennifer Marsh. She can't get her novels published, so she does what any twenty-nine-year-old part-time caterer who watches too many talk shows and lives in Macon, Georgia, would do. She devises a plan to commit murder. She'll be arrested, and her name will be splashed across the media. Within a week—two, tops—her ironclad alibi will surface, she'll be exonerated, and she will become the media's latest literary darling. She'll be published and her books will sell wildly.

It's a great plan, but it's doomed from the start. Jennifer's a good Southern Baptist girl. She could never murder anyone, but, unfortunately, someone else could. Jennifer finds herself accused of a murder she didn't commit and trapped in her own harebrained scheme. But she is not alone. Her allies include a good-looking investigative re-porter, an eccentric writers' group, and a band of little old ladies who have a nose for sleuthing, and a pet that may or may not be a dog.

Q. Janet Evanovich endorsed Dying to Get Published *as "bracingly perceptive about the realities of book publishing in the 1990s." Considering this is your first published novel, how did you come by your insider information?*

A. The one-word answer is: *painfully.* I don't have as many rejections as Jennifer (I'm not as obsessed with writing as she is), but I've certainly had my share of both form letters and the "I like this, but I don't *love* it" letters. And everyone who writes has agent stories.

Also, for the past several years, I've been involved with local writers' groups, attended conferences and retreats, and listened to what people in the business—writers (both pub-lished and unpublished), agents, editors—have to say. They all have tales, and they all have suggestions.

Q. What inspired you to create Jennifer Marsh?

A. Jennifer was obviously born out of frustration, but I also had a simple idea: How far would a good person go to achieve what she wants (or, at least, *thinks* she wants) most out of life?

I wrote thirteen pages of the novel and took them to a weekly writers' group that I had been invited to join. I didn't think the book would be marketable—it broke a lot of rules—let alone that it might develop into a series. The group read it, loved it, and insisted that I write it. I'm not sure they thought I could sell it, but they all wanted to read it.

Q. We're also interested in some of the other characters who will reappear alongside Jennifer. Could you tell us about Jennifer's writers' critique group? Are the members based on actual people?

A. Jennifer belongs to a writers' group that meets every Monday night. (And Jennifer will be there every Monday, without fail, as long as there is breath in her body.) Monique is the fortyish matriarch of the group who, because she's older than the rest and has one published science fiction novel to her credit, assumes a condescending, teacher role. The others, like Jennifer, are in their mid-to-late twenties. Petite Leigh Ann lives and breathes romance, Teri writes romantic suspense, and perpetually pregnant April is into children's books.

My own writers' group vehemently denies any similarities to Jennifer's, but they are extremely talented and professional people. Three of the six of us are now published and the others, I have no doubt, will be as soon as they are fortunate enough to find editors who fall in love with the stories they want to tell.

Q. How would you describe your personal writing process? Do you have a specific routine? A desired daily page count? A weekly goal in terms of production?

A. Once I find my story, I set a goal of two *usable* pages a day or ten pages a week or fifty pages a month. Usually I write more than that, but life has a tendency to interfere, and writing is something that can't be faked—like looking busy when the boss comes by. Establishing higher goals only adds more pressure in what is already a high-pressure business. I try to write for four or five hours in the morning, but once I'm really into a book, ideas come at odd times, like the middle of the night, and I'm always jotting down notes so I won't forget them. When I was writing the sequel to *Dying to Get Published,* I awoke out of a dead sleep at about five o'clock one morning knowing whodunit. But I never push a plot. If it's not coming, I stop writing until I'm sure what should happen next. And I rewrite constantly.

Q. What's in the immediate (and, if you care to discuss it, long-range) future for Jennifer and her friends?

A. In the second Jennifer Marsh book, *Dying to Get Even,* Emma Walker, Jennifer's dear little old lady friend from *Dying to Get Published,* is accused of murdering her ex-husband, Edgar. Unfortunately, Jennifer turns out to be the primary witness against her, having seen Mrs. Walker holding the murder weapon over Edgar's dead body. Jennifer feels personally responsible for the case against her friend, and she, with help from newspaper reporter Sam Culpepper and fellow writers Leigh Ann, Teri, April, and Monique, must find a way to get Mrs. Walker exonerated.

The third book is in its infancy and may change, so I won't talk about it at this point. It was difficult choosing which adventure to take Jennifer on next. Wherever life leads her, I'm sure Sam and the writers' group will be there to help her out of the predicaments she manages to get herself into.

Q. Now that you've completed two books in the Jennifer Marsh series (and have embarked upon the third), what would you say are the particular challenges of writing series characters?

A. I think an author has to strike a balance between keeping characters consistent and letting them grow and develop. Also, people get attached to some of the supporting characters and want to see them come back in other books, so it becomes a balancing act, using some familiar characters while introducing new ones.

Q. This is the year you moved from "pre-published" to published. Do you have any advice for novice writers, those real-life Jennifer Marshes, who want to achieve what you have?

A. My best advice is don't give up, learn your trade, and never view a rejection as a reflection on your talent. I believe that the story is what sells a book, but good writing is essential. Finding an editor who wants to publish the story a writer wants to tell requires a lot of research and a lot of luck.

A novice writer has to decide if she or he is in this business for the long haul, because for many of us who have been published, it took years to reach that goal. Persistence is every bit as important as talent. Writing and marketing are not for the fainthearted.

I think I became a true professional when I finally put aside my first book and started something totally different. *Dying to Get Published* was the third book I wrote, and the first to be published. I would suggest that writers keep trying new ideas, new characters, and new ways to tell their stories until they find a "voice" that works for them and for an editor.

One word of caution: Never write a sequel until you've sold the first one. Time would be better spent developing a new concept. When an editor buys your book, he or she will give you time to write the second.

Most important, break all the rules. It worked for me.